The Priestess

Amethyst Gray

To Chris + Becki
Enjoy!
Amethyst x

Dedicated to all those affected by, or lost as a result of, the COVID-19 Pandemic of 2020

Contents

Forward

This book is a short story made of two intertwined destinies of very touching and soulful heroes. It is light and joyful, while profound and tragic as well.

It comes at a fascinating time when the Earth and the Human Race are facing today very similar challenges.
Atlantis on the one side, crystal skulls on the other. Two fascinating subjects. The legend says that the skulls were given to us by twelve races of frequent visitors from space who wanted to help in our development.

I was told the same story from four independent sources, from three different continents. It is a deeply rooted legend or story. The first book I ever read was a famous Belgian comic strip named the Atlantis Enigma.

At 64, my lust to know more about Atlantis is as strong as ever! If you have this book in your hand, there is a fair chance that you are one of those people who want to know, as I do, more about Atlantis. The "more" you will find here is delicious soul food — the same with the skulls. The original twelve/thirteen skulls are deep, positive and powerful beings.

Amethyst Gray gives us some lovely insights from a time when the skulls were the very backbone of Atlantis. An unexpected threat suddenly appeared, and I will not say any more and let Amethyst tell you the rest.

Why are stories such as Avatar, Harry Potter and Star Wars so popular? Because they are modern fairy tales with positive values which give us recipes and courage to face the uncertain and challenging times we are facing. Far beyond the rational and scientific paradigms, they speak about energies, about facing together the unknown, about "the Force being with us", The same applies to this book and gives it delicious and precious energy.

The reader will feel Amethyst's experience in meditation, Reiki healing and a way of being where spiritual energy is essential. Enjoy!

Philippe Ullens

Prologue

Acclaimed Archaeologist Doctor Diana Garry from Bath Sulis University in South West England had made a name for herself on her recent dig at the Chateau of Chenonceau in the Loire Valley of France.

Wanting a new challenge and a free holiday she had agreed to undertake an excavation around a partially submerged pile of rocks on the south side of South Bimini island in the Bahamas.

The rock pile was not so far from the so-called 'Bimini Road' feature that some say was linked to Atlantis. Still, the road was more likely a later feature, such as a quayside, created before the water-level rose as far as it had in recent millennia around the island.

Whatever she found, she was determined to act with integrity and let the evidence speak for itself. If it were just a pile of rocks, she'd pack up and go home early. If it were Phoenician, as she hoped, then that would be a big deal. And if it were Atlantean – well that would change the history of the world forever.

'there was an island situated in front of the straits which are by you called the Pillars of Heracles [Gibraltar]*; the island was larger than Libya and Asia put together...this island of Atlantis'* Plato: Timaeus

A slim figure in a flowing blue robe gently bathed alongside a pod of dolphins in a seawater pool under a roof of dazzling crystals. Her hands were hovering over the form of an injured man whose limp body was floating on a small raft half-submerged in the water. Her concentration focussed on a clear blue crystal skull resting on a plinth beside the pool as she chanted in an an-

cient language. The Priestess was determined to heal this dying man.

I – Aftermath

"Oh, bother!"

Diana Garry, Doctor of Archaeology at Bath Sulis University, famously associated with finding Roman mosaic pavements in France, was feeling particularly nauseous today.

It was now the start of her third month living on a boat.

The beautiful Bahamas had been devastated by hurricane Dorian, so the original plans for a luxurious stay in a hotel on shore had been changed to a hastily chartered tour boat with onboard cabins and dining facilities. The alternative had been to cancel the whole dig, but as funding would be lost and the academics had already missed their chance to find alternative posts they decided to continue.

One of the interesting aspects of the hurricane damage had been the amount of ground that had been disturbed by the waves and powerful winds. The target site was vastly different to how it had appeared in the original survey. Now impressive marble boulders and partial pillars were poking up above ground rather than requiring to be dug.

But Diana wasn't enjoying that part at the moment anyway. She was trying to keep her food down in the heavy swell. Thankfully she could spend much of the day ashore with her team digging and recording on-site. Many of her team members were from the Atlantic University of Miami. As ever they were very green young undergraduates on their first trip away from home. But they were generally keen and slightly bemused by such seemingly western cultural features such as Doric columns in a Caribbean setting. The differing pronunciation by her North American colleagues always amused her. She was sure that 'Caribbean' only contained 2 'b's.

Some local game fishermen had alerted the archaeological community to these 'Ancient Greek' remains just offshore a year or so earlier. These had been taken as tall tales by most people. But an anonymous entrepreneur – rumoured to be Edward Dusk – had offered to fund a dig to prove or disprove an old-world presence in the new-world by examining the remains. That same entrepreneur had requested Diana's involvement after reading about her exploits at the chateau of Chenonceau in the Loire Valley of France.

On the face of it, the chance to dig in the Bahamas to dismiss a ludicrous assertion that the Greeks had visited there had seemed like an easy assignment for a fantastic holiday that she could never afford. But some of the dating evidence sent away for testing had sparked some controversy by coming back matching the late Bronze age. The style of the columns also appeared more Phoenician than ancient Greek or Roman. It was an enigma.

Her father had sparked more controversy by telling the press locally in the UK that she had gone to dig on the site of Atlantis. Good old Pop. The local government antiquities department had almost pulled their permission to dig over that. But Diana had been quick to allay their fears by demonstrating that the evidence was from the old world not from a sunken city. At least in the layer she was currently digging.

Stanislav Havel, her assistant once again, had gone over to the Lebanese coast to examine the hypothesis that the finds they had made in South Bimini were Phoenician. Diana was missing him already.

"Oh Stan, I hope you get the permits to examine the remains near Tyre quickly." She said under her breath.

$\mathcal{II}$ – Finds

"**D**octor Garry, Doctor Garry, we found something. It looks metallic Miss."

The unmistakable southern drawl of Jerry, one of the mature students from New Orleans who had been seconded to the team from the Atlantic University of Miami, awoke Diana from her thoughts of Stan in the Lebanon.

"Hi there, Jerry. We have yet to find anything metallic on site. Are you sure it's not a piece of shell or pottery glaze?"

"No, Miss. It's definitely metallic. Marla reckons it must have been included in the building in some tarred sackcloth. The brittle cloth just peeled off a piece to expose it to us. It even looks like gold or brass. Come look-see."

Diana sighed. She put down her coffee mug and picked up her makeup brush set and manicure accessories. None of it was for the vanity. The tools were ideal for carefully exposing delicate finds. So far, nothing had required them as it had been masonry. But, potential cloth with its carbon dating possibilities and worked metal was possible primary and secondary dating evidence.

Diana quietly but briskly followed the elegant blonde to the find site. Jerry was a big fan of Marilyn Monroe and was wearing a sun top that was inspired by her heroine.

"Here Miss. I have kept the tar cloth to one side. Is that an eye?"

Sure enough, the metallic item did appear to have an eye peeking out. She laid a ruler next to the find and took a couple of shots of the discovery using her digital SLR camera with GPS.

Recording finds in situ was part of the job.

Diana handed Jerry a makeup brush while she set to work with her cuticle trimmer to brush away centuries of debris from the object.

Quite rapidly, the artefact was exposed to both of the archaeologists.

"Well, Jerry, that is incredible."

Jerry nodded. Diana took another couple of photographs of the object. It appeared very strongly to be a small statuette of a deity of some kind made in a type of brass. The dating of the wrapping and a small sample together with spectroscopy should say what type.

"Miss Diana, I mean Doctor, it looks kinda like Poseidon. It has a fishy gill head and the stump where a trident might have gone. I saw one in a museum once. I think it was Greek or Phoenician. I forget which."

"You might be right, Jerry. When we get it back to the boat, we can whisk it to the lab. Is it loose now?"

"I think so. If you want I can put it in the finds box and take it. I was about to go off for lunch."

"OK. I will call it through to Sta. I mean Dean. He can run the tests and use the satellite link to check it against known similar artefacts. "

"Yes, ma'am. I just love this dig!"

Diana knew this was a significant find. But what did it prove? Pre-Columbus contact between the ancient world and the new world? For sure. But who and why? Father Crespi had claimed a similar link nearly half a century before. But his treasures were seemingly lost. They had no confirmed source and were sometimes of dubious quality. We would never know for sure about them. But this was undisturbed under ancient ruins for centuries. This find might settle the question. But such a leap away from the standard textbooks needed to be good. So any checks had to be thorough.

Diana returned to her tepid coffee cup in the incident tent at the edge of the beach to continue her paperwork and avoid lunchtime without Stan.

It was around 3 pm that Dean excitedly called her up on the team walkie-talkie.

"Diana. I mean Doctor Garry. You will never guess what? The statuette. It's old. Too old really. "

"Calm down, Dean. How old?"

"The sample says around 4,500 years old. I rechecked it four times."

"Wow. I wasn't expecting that. Can we send samples to Miami and London to be sure?"

"Of course. I also got spectroscopy on the metal. It is brass or possibly orichalcum."

"Excuse me. What?"

"Orichalcum. It was found off of Italy in a sunken Greek ship a few years ago. Our sample matches the ingots the team found there within 1% of constituents. And the statue itself is similar to those found in the Mediterranean around the Bronze Age. "

"Amazing. That is exciting news. Thanks, Dean. I will report this to base."

"Yes, Ma'am".

Diana turned on her laptop to search 'orichalcum'. It was widely mentioned in ancient times but also linked by Plato in his 'Critias' work that recalls Atlantis. Poseidon, the deity that could be the subject of the statuette was also linked to Atlantis. The Island she was excavating on was also in the Atlantic Ocean 'beyond the pillars of Heracles', as Plato had stated – I.e. beyond Gibraltar. Thankfully, she was way beyond Gibraltar, and the date of 4,500 years of age did not match up with the ten or eleven thousand years also mentioned by Plato.

"Coincidence. I am not going back down Alice's rabbit hole again. This find is probably proof of an ancient trading outpost from a Mediterranean power. Nothing more." She muttered to herself.

She decided to call up Stan despite the late hour to see if he had any reassurances for her. She tried calling him, but it just went to voice mail. Both he and she were out of coverage areas, so it wasn't a surprise. She just wanted to hear his voice before she reported this to Miami.

III – Miami

The Archaeological director at the Atlantic University of Miami, Professor Chuck Morris, was very traditional in his thinking. The approach by the anonymous benefactor had come at a critical time for his department's resources, but searching for proof of Atlantis hadn't been what he would have chosen. Two years from retirement he wanted no-nonsense messing up his pension pot.

It was with that thinking which had caused him to approach the University of Bath Sulis to engage Doctor Diana Garry. She had accomplished great things in France and avoided unnecessary negative publicity for her quite controversial findings. She also had an outspoken maverick father that she somehow managed to keep in check, so seemed ideal for Mr Dusk's poisoned chalice – if indeed he was the anonymous benefactor. Though with a separate expedition team recruited to investigate Antarctica for hidden technologies by the same benefactor it seemed likely. In an off the record interview that Chuck had been given access to it would seem that this particular billionaire was convinced that Nikola Tesla had previously either lived in Atlantis or had 'channelled' his inventions from there. It didn't matter if that was the case or not as it was the man's belief that triggered these projects. Hopefully just like himself as a respected archaeologist Doctor Garry could be relied upon to avoid sensationalism.

So the phone call from Diana Garry notifying him of the latest find wasn't quite the news that he wanted. But thankfully they both agreed that the early bronze age finds required further rigorous analysis before any conclusions were made public.

"Good girl." Something to report back to the benefactor to keep the funds coming in, but not enough to blow open the legend of Atlantis. More likely Greek or Phoenician.

As a young man at a well-known institution, he had assisted his lead archaeologist in destroying giant skeletons found in Native American mound burial sites. The presence of such remains was an inconvenience to the various theories of the origin of man. He still felt a tinge of guilt at what he had done. But at the time he had believed it was for the greater good. Now he wasn't so sure. It seemed like it was just destroying primary evidence to defend an outdated dogma. Now he was part of that dogma he could see how the status quo kept itself in place. But he was also now happy to push the boundaries a little. He could live with an old-world trading post on his doorstep. It might even satisfy the nut jobs who hailed the Bimini pavement as proof of Atlantis. Well, maybe it was just an old Greek or Phoenician port. He never liked Columbus Day anyway.

IV – Dreamtime

The excitement of the day over it was time to pack up her belongings and jump on the speedboat to the ship. The old boat was comfortable enough and had scuba facilities. According to Diana's sources, this was one of Jacques Cousteau's old *Calypso* ships from the 1970s, Now renamed as the *Nostradamus* and registered in Panama.

The gangway wasn't fantastic, but Diana had yet to slip into the water – even in rough weather. Today there was a slight swell, and the waves were raising the rear of the tender up and down while the *Nostradamus* pitched and yawed back and forth. But with a careful leap, Diana crossed onto the gangway and climbed the stairs onto the deck. One of the deckhands was having a smoke as she made her way along the planking towards the stern where the archaeologists were staying. The only other Brit on board, Rupert, was taking pictures of the sunset as she reached the door to the cabins. He was a personable individual, a little bit shy, but a whizz with the geophysics equipment. It had been he who had recalibrated the machine to deal with the water-soaked sand below the dig site. It had hampered further investigation since the transmitter and receiver units were somewhat old and unsuited to the environment. Still, Rupert had made the best of it and produced useful plots of possible wall structures below the collapsed columns.

"Evening, Diana. Have you had a good day? I hear we found some metal icon earlier. Anything exciting?"

"Hi, Rupert. Not bad thanks. The find could be crucial to the context of the site, but it is hard to know. Small religious items can often be found out of context in structures simply as offerings to the local gods. I will be happier with more datable finds attached or in the walls. You know, shells, seeds and carbon deposits. Boring to look at but oh so valuable for us as archaeologists. But the pretty finds are what the public wants of course. How about you?"

"I reckon I can rig up the underwater drone to give us a LIDAR scan of the seabed when we next have a calm day. If you will allow me to deploy our little toy."

"Oh, for sure. Sounds fantastic. "

Diana wandered down to her cabin. She opened the door and set her bag down onto the large bunk she shared with her husband. It had been an exciting day. It made the concept of an Atlantis more plausible, but not in the classic Plato timeframe. Yet. She sighed and went over to the sink to freshen up. She wondered what the chef would be dishing up tonight. His lasagne was quite excellent. But some of his concoctions were, well, odd. Sausage tandoori, Chinese tortillas and sweet and sour boiled eggs all came to mind.

She quickly changed her top and wandered up to the ship's galley. There the faded 1980's decor made her think about big hair and shoulder pads. She chuckled at one of her early memories of Aunt Hilda with her outfits inspired by Elaine Paige from a number of her hit shows in the West End theatre district of London. With her season tickets to Lloyd-Webber shows, Aunt Hilda was their number one superfan. I was just a shame that she had similarly been a big fan of gin which had killed her. "I know him so well". She burst into a quiet song at the thought.

"Excuse me?"

"Oh sorry, Tommy, I was deep in thought."

"That's OK ma'am. I know you Brits like your music. I grew up with Oasis, Blur and Pulp myself. Oh and the Spice Girls. If you wanna be my lover..." He ended on a reprise of the Spice Girl song.

"Ah, yes. Lovely." She sounded somewhat unconvinced. It was probably his deep resonance, southern drawl and flat tone that spoilt it for her.

Just then Chef banged his dinner gong.

"Listen up, folks. We got Thai Mussaman curry gator balls or nut roast for you vegetable people. Don't pour the cheesy sauce if you're vegans. "

So, another strange combination. Diana had eaten both Mussaman curry – one of her favourites in fact – and gator balls. But never in the same dish. It could be another interesting experience. Thankfully she had her charcoal tablets with her if it didn't agree with her tummy.

She took her tray, grabbed a knife and fork plus a glass of apple juice. The chef served out her plate and gave her a cheeky smile. She smiled back. His leathery skin and missing tooth made him look like he was in his 70's rather than his rumoured 55 years.

She carried her tray over to one of the bench tables. There she made some small talk with her dig ladies while savouring Chef's latest dish. It was quite tasty if a little odd in its texture.

Around 9 pm, she excused herself and headed back to her cabin. It had been a long day and was catching up with her.

Back in her cabin, she brushed her teeth, changed into her nightie and climbed into bed. The earlier sea swell had calmed now it was dark, and she was soon breathing in tune with the up and down movements of the ship. The dreaming started and took her to a long time ago, not so very far away.

She saw a large book in front of her that had to be an Atlas of sorts with a strange flag on the front of it. That was on a white background with a red cross on the front with the tops of the crosses each divided up into three waves. Each of the arms of the cross was connected by the quadrant of a circle in black. The book was entitled the 'Chronicles of Atlantis'.

And as she went further into the darkness, the book became

sharper in focus before she fell into it. And as she did so, she could read that the book was about a priestess who had lived a long time ago in a nearby continent with an advanced civilisation called Atlantis. Its empire extended from the tip of Peru in the south-west to Alaska in the northwest through to Archangel in the northeast to the top of Africa and Madagascar then encompassing most of Arabia and the Mediterranean.

The three-pronged trident of Poseidon signified the rule of the three continents of America, Atlantis and Africa. The shield of Atlantis was an equilateral cross on a circular background that represented the island of Atlantis' four rivers flowing north, east, west and south - the original Tibor, Rhine, Euphrates and Nile. Its capital, Atlán, nestled beneath the hook headed Mount Olympus with its majestic slopes.

The Pyramid of the Light - dedicated to the Sun deity rose majestically over the capital, its shadow eclipsing one side or the other of the bridges crossing the concentric circles of the holy island or its surrounding canals. The histories of the peoples of Atlantis were spoken of all over the globe. It's ultimate decline, fall and fiery, wet destruction faded from history to become a legend and finally a myth. The Atlantic Ocean, first muddy and shallow then wide and deep still bears its name but little else. No living memory of that vibrant culture remains.

𝒱 - Perfect Day

When she awoke from her deep sleep, she discovered that Stan had returned from Lebanon and was now lying beside her in their double bunk. She leant over and kissed him before they embraced for a moment of passion.

At breakfast, the French toast went down nicely. Diana was disappointed to hear from Stan that the Doric columns from the dig were distinctly different from all known examples in Phoenician settlements as well as differing from Roman and Greek columns too. Though there were standard features their dig column shared with all of them. Almost as if it predated them all. She rapidly dropped that thought as she recalled her dream from the night before—surely stress. Renaissance France was one thing, but Atlantis was something else. She might as well have been dreaming of a life in Middle Earth with Hobbits or Elves.

"Stan, as it is the weekend, I think we need a day or two off together. I can ask Jerry to call me up if anything comes up. We can both perhaps sleep ashore in one of the beach huts at the edge of the dig site and chill out in the pleasant weather. What do you think my love?"

"That's a great idea. Let's grab our sleeping things, plus my fishing spear and catch some fish for supper. I need to unwind after Tyre and Beirut. I am still a bit jet-lagged. "

"I will bring some water along. And maybe an aperitif or two."

At the beach, the two lovers carried their bedding and bottles over to one of the few remaining beach structures to survive hurricane Dorian.

The beach hut was quite small, but cosy and cool away from the bright Caribbean sunshine. There was a wide bunk, hinge-fronted wall and a cool box to place the drinks in. Stan put the bedding roll on the bunk while Diana put the wine and the pastis into the cool box. The shabby decor with a faded and very dated poster of Madonna indicated that the last time the hut had been decorated was in the 1980s. Stan laughed as the 'Material Girl' in her 'Like a Virgin' album cover's wedding dress was now resplendent with a Joseph Stalin style moustache.

With their supplies stowed Stan took his fishing rod and hooked on a piece of bread he had pocketed at breakfast. He cast off with all the expertise you would expect from a seasoned fisherman with an Uncle who owned a fishing boat still actively trawling along the rivers of Czechia.

Diana placed her beach towel down on the secluded stretch of sand. She loosened her bathing skirt and let it drop to the ground to reveal her bikini bottoms. She then tugged off her tee-shirt to reveal her simple yet modest bikini top. She tutted to herself as she looked down towards her waist to see a bit more of a stomach than she was expecting to see. "Those darn pancakes and maple syrup."

She lay down on her beach towel to enjoy the golden rays of the Caribbean sunshine. Stan had managed to catch some type of carp, which he smashed against a rock before putting it in an old bucket of seawater. He carried it up to the hut and placed it in the cool box before heading back down to where his wife was dozing in the sun. A cheeky grin flicked across his face before he lent down over Diana to put his cold, wet hands on her hot shoulders.

"Stan! What the... You git. I can't believe you did that."

He ran down the beach towards the water's edge as Diana ran after him in hot pursuit. As soon as he was deep enough, he turned to splash her.

"No, you don't." She half screamed at him. Then she half-submerged herself before retaliating with a volley of water back in his direction.

"No fair! You are much better at splashing than me. I had to catch our supper!"

"He who lives in glass houses should not throw stones. I got you back!"

They both laughed hysterically until Stan swept her up in his arms to carry her back into the beach hut. A little bit of 'afternoon delight' was in order as they embraced gently before settling back onto the bunk bed together.

Around an hour later the couple emerged from their temporary home. Stan picked up his rod, popped another piece of bread on to its hook and cast off once more. Diana decided to freshen up with a swim a little away from the fishing rod.

The water was refreshing after the heat they had generated together and the outside air temperature. Diana swam parallel to the beach towards the dig site. She waved at Jerry, who was sitting to chat with one of the local men who had been assisting with sifting the soil and taking it away from the area. Jerry waved back, winking and smiling. It seemed that archaeology was not the main thing on her mind this weekend.

As Diana turned away from the dig site to swim back, the image of two dolphins entered her mind. Just as she looked up towards the direction she was swimming; she glimpsed two dolphins splashing up ahead of her. Another case of synchronicity. She swam back on toward Stan who was standing on the shore by the beach hut.

Once in front of her beach towel, she put her feet down and walked up on to the shore, gesturing to Stan that she would splash him if he tried to splash her again. She shook her shoulder-length hair and sat down on her towel, admiring the view and her husband.

As she lay down to sleep in the early afternoon spring sunlight, she began to dream.

She saw her father – not the father she had in this lifetime- lying limp in her arms, with dolphins swimming around her, and a cave of crystals above her head as she bathed in a large, warm seawater pool. The pain and pent up anger she felt was palpable. "Father, no. Why, why!"

When Stan woke her up an hour or so later, Diana was more than a little disorientated. "Father!" she cried. Stan replied. "No, he's in England. You spoke to him last night. You are with me, Stan on South Bahama island."

"Bahama? Atlán?" She replied.

"Diana, stop messing with me. "

Diana snapped out of her trance and glanced at her husband.

"That was some dream I just had. I wonder what it means."

She recounted the details of her dream as Stan listened open-mouthed. "Not again, my love, surely?"

Stan had caught enough fish, so started on gutting them while Diana set to work collecting wood for the fire over which to cook the catch. With all the flotsam that had been loosened by Hurricane Dorian, the task was relatively easy. With Stan's boy scout skills with lighting a fire and Diana's cooking abilities from her many camping trips with her family around Dorset and the West Country of England the fish was soon sizzling away on its multiple spits.

When the food was ready, the couple devoured it with arms entwined, trying to repeat the romantic scene from 'Lady and the Tramp' but without the pasta. They laughed and cried as they easily ate their barbecued carp.

Afterwards, Diana and Stan watched the sunset together sat on the beach arm in arm, occasionally kissing and soaking up the atmosphere of a Caribbean spring evening. It was idyllic.

"Shall we have a moonlight dip my love?" Asked Diana.

"Definitely!"

The lovers ran into the sea hand in hand, splashing their way through the surf.

They were swimming away from each other when a pair of jet skis rounded the headland. Diana just glimpsed the inner one as it hit her head with a glancing blow.

Everything went dark.

As Diana succumbed to the darkness, she saw herself falling into the large book she had seen before. As the light returned to her eyes, her form had changed into that of a woman in a blue robe. Nothing looked familiar to her, and yet...

VI - Messima

Messima, daughter of Oriel, Priestess of the Light and the Water lives in the city of Medina on its southern tip above the rocky cliffs at the entrance to the Nile on the western side. Her residence is the Tower of the Light and the Water – a modest yet imposing structure with unobstructed views of the South Atlantic to the south and the plains of Atlán to the north.

The Priesthood is forbidden to marry but often takes companions. Messima's companion, her concubine, is Néma. The petite olive-skinned, brown-headed, brown-eyed, concubine contrasted strikingly with the tall, slim, pale blonde-headed, 35-year-old Priestess. Bonded by trust Néma in her pure white robe often accompanies Messima on her journeys in her aquamarine robe adorned with symbolic gold right bracelet and left anklet.

Medina is very much a provincial town, unimportant in the vastness of Atlantis, but a renowned centre of healing. As a priestess of the light and the water, healing is Messima's principal role. Beneath the white pinnacle of the tower is a vast warren of caverns accessed via a deep spiral staircase with accesses off at different angles and different depths. The two main healing chambers are the dry chamber and the wet chamber. The large dry chamber, with its imposing 100-metre diameter aquamarine crystal-encrusted roof 30 metres high at its height point with its great resonance is ideal for sound healing with light and the crystals themselves. The smaller wet chamber with its cosier 30-metre diameter and the 20-metre-high amethyst crystal-encrusted surface is partly submerged with sea water-filled through subterranean tunnels leading out to the South Atlantic. Through the tubes come the dolphin healers powerful with their range of knowledge on acoustics and resonant balance. The dolphin visitors are mainly bottlenose dolphins.

Messima's favourite task is to swim with the dolphins and share in the healing process of another patient in the warm and refreshing ocean pool. But on this occasion, she took little pleasure in the swim. As she dried herself and dressed back in her robe, her memory kept going back to events of the previous week.

It had all started as a simple piece of rebalancing of her father's light body. She had taken him into the dry chamber with her three apprentice priests and priestesses. They had performed the prescribed healing ritual. The resonance had been good, and Oriel had responded well. But there had been an extra, deeper resonance that Messima had not sensed before. She dismissed it as a probable earth tremor elsewhere on the island, but her unease was palpable.

The next day Oriel had gone into a rapid decline. His body had been limp, and even with the help of her dolphin friends in the wet chamber, she had been unable to save him. His passing into the shadows had been unstoppable. Despite Néma's comforting Messima's sorrow had been insuperable. She blamed herself for his death.

VII – The Funeral

Oriel had been a dignitary in the area around Medina. The Mayor himself had insisted that the main ante-chamber of the major town meeting house be made available for her father's eulogy and wake.

In Atlantean tradition, the bell of the ancestors of her family was rung as the funeral procession carried Oriel's body in its open-topped casket from her family home to the meeting house. Crowds of well-wishers lined the streets throwing and dropping poppies, lilies and scented roses on to the coffin. Oriel had been a just, noble and generous man in his life, and the people of Medina were responding to his death.

As family matriarch upon her mother's and aunt's deaths, the task of reading the eulogy fell to Messima. With crowds gathered in the meeting house and eyes streaming with tears, Messima read to the expectant throng. Using her Priestley calming technique, she was able to begin. "Oriel, my father, was a great but gentle man. We look forward to his next incarnation. My family have lost a loved one here on Atlantis, but we have gained a star in the heavens. Praise to the deity who gives us all of our sustenance. Amun-Ra". The people all responded with "Amun-Ra".

The funeral gong sounded outside to indicate the start of the wake. Messima found the whole wake experience both upsetting and strangely uplifting at the same time. Many friends and neighbours of her father had held him in such high regard. Yet she had become more distant from him since she had joined the priesthood. Now nearly twenty years later she regretted the many upsets since her happy family upbringing. It was far too late in this lifetime.

All too soon, it seemed to her; the funeral gong sounded again. Messima hurried to the door of the meeting house to lead the procession out of the town to the small hilltop where a funeral pyre would be lit. Again, the well-wishers who were not following the casket were lining the street. Walls of people in their brightly coloured and shimmering white robes masked the shining white walls of the buildings in the town.

The low, flat rooves of the settlement had been here for aeons, yet the rich autumnal sun made everything seem bright and new. As the casket passed them the bystanders turned their faces and backs to the body as a mark of respect.

The procession wound its way along the twisty lane that led to the hilltop. As Oriel's body took its final journey towards the fire, the Priestess could see the pile of wood for the funeral pyre. Néma moved forward and briefly clasped Messima's hand before dropping back behind the casket. At last, they arrived. The casket bearers scooped up and placed Oriel's body onto the funeral pyre.

Messima, as The Priestess of the Light and the Waters, anointed her father's face and limbs with a profusion of olive oil, lavender and herbs.

She turned to the crowd and taking the lit torch, exalted "Now I return to the light - Amun-Ra".

She took the torch and lit the four corners of the woodpile. As she did so, the Sun began to set in the West, and the flames overtook the shape of Oriel's body.

The family and close friends of Oriel stayed around the funeral pyre singing traditional songs of great deeds and magical journeys from the past. As the flames died down a torch was lit from the pyre to light the small fire where a lamb was to be spit-roasted for the final feast. The festivities and the formal process went on until dawn.

At first light, the remains of the funeral pyre could be seen. The ashes - still warm - were swept up using yew tree brooms and put into a funeral vase. Once all the ashes were swept up, and the jar was full, it was lifted on to the saddle of the grey donkey - as was traditional.

The remaining funeral party members gave their leave of Messima. They then headed back towards Medina. Only Néma remained with the Priestess and the donkey as they prepared for the trek towards the wood where Oriel's ashes were to be scattered. Néma hugged her companion as they both set off northwards

VIII - The Woods

I t was with some relief that the donkey finally arrived at the edge of the woods. The searing heat of a glorious autumn day had sapped at Messima's strength. Now nearly midday the green-brown foliage of the oak woods provided a refreshing sanctuary for the Priestess and her companion. Pausing briefly under the dappled canopy the two women drank fresh water from a leather bottle while the donkey drank from a slow running brook.

"Only a little way to go now" whispered Messima - her words broken up by a cuckoo announcing its presence.

"It is just as well. You look terrible." Said Néma.

"Thanks" responded Messima. It was true. The ceremonies, funeral pyre and long trek, had all taken their toll on her. Messima's best robe was now covered in a thin layer of dust; her blonde hair was tangled and matted, her face had a slight touch of soot, except under her hazel-brown eyes where tears had washed it away. Néma had fared somehow better. Her white robe was still bright, the corded sash around her slim waist, providing a sharp contrast.

"Here, let me fix you up a bit". Néma gently took out a small piece of cloth, poured a tiny amount of water onto it and gently mopped her companion's face. "That's better."

"Thanks, Ne.".

Ten minutes later, the path widened out into a clearing. A gentle rushing sound of water filled the air and grew louder as the party neared their destination – Rainbow Falls. Not large by any means but not diminished in their beauty the falls helped to drain Lake Komo as the water made its way to join the Nile several metres lower down. The lake itself, although not visible from below the falls, formed a natural break in the vast Atlantean escarpment to the north of Medina into the south of the capital Atlán. Rainbow Falls marked the lake's south-east tip. The falls dropped some 20 to 25 metres into a plunge pool surrounded by the forest clearing in the Great Woods. Around the plunge pool, large boulders deposited by the last ice age provided seats for the companions to rest upon.

After a brief pause, Messima stood up. "It is time". She said. As she was unsealing the top of the funeral vase, she started to hum. Néma joined in as the two friends walked around the edge of the clearing. The Priestess gently shook the contents – Oriel's ashes – so that they caught the slight breeze and were spread all around the clearing and into the edge of the woods. When the vase was empty, she took it and smashed it against one of the central rocks in the clearing. Then she took a small pointed spade out from the donkey's saddlebag and proceeded to bury the broken vase under the edge of the rock. "It is done. Praise to the deity. Thanks to Gaia. Amun-Ra."

"Amun-Ra" echoed Néma.

The ceremony over, the two women disrobed and plunged straight into the pool below the falls. It was good for Messima to unwind after the last two days.

Néma gently embraced her friend to show her that she was not on her own. After diving, splashing and frolicking, it was nearly time to head back.

Drying off on towels from the saddlebag, the companions ate simple snacks of fruits and biscuits with hard cheese. Then they tapped the donkey to start the journey back.

IX – The Adventure

Messima and Néma returned the donkey to its stable and arrived back at their home. The tall tower with its white-sanded walls stood out from the dusky skyline. The beacon on an islet just out to sea was already shining brightly, its crystal globe warning approaching ships of the dangerous cliffs, the rocks and approaches to the mouth of the Nile. A crystal cutter laden with tea, cotton or spices was racing the darkness as its Captain manoeuvred the ship into position to enter the channel through the cliffs.

Weary from their travels, the friends unbolted the door and entered the base of the tower. The crystal lights increased their glow as the two companions went inside. Messima retired to her meditation room to relax while Néma performed her duties in preparing herbal tea. Néma placed the rosemary, jasmine and camomile infusion into two large obsidian beakers, their oversized saucer acting as handles as she picked them up in turn and filled them with natural hot spring water (a significant advantage that volcanic Atlantis held over many other parts of the world). She took the beaker to her mistress and sat beside her. Their official status spoke little of their real relationship.

Messima sat in a near Lotus position on a thick mat of woven hemp on the white marble floor. Behind her, the nearly human-sized quartz crystal generator was starting to pulse in violet, green and indigo hues as the Priestess made contact with it. Soon she was in a deep trance - images of days passed mingling with those of the future. One picture and voice stood out amongst the rest.

Marnon was Messima's paternal cousin who lived with her

uncle Joslin on Atlantis Minor. The colonies had been a popular destination for many Atlanteans. Still, the southern island with its strange animals such as penguins, toucans and wild elephant herds were popular with naturalists such as her uncle. Messima had holidayed there several times in her youth. Now Marnon had decided to contact her to give her his condolences no doubt and more family gossip. Thinking his name loudly in her mind, his voice came through crystal clear.

"Sorry to hear about Unc. Now his brother's acting oddly - can you come down here and see what's up - we would love to have you. And yes, 'She' can come."

Messima responded with her greeting and her agreement to come straight away but snorted as she broke contact. Unwinding from her trance, she took hold of her beaker and took a large sip.

"Ne, we are going away. We are seeing Marnon."

"Great" replied Néma sarcastically. She knew that Marnon was jealous of her relationship with Messima and didn't approve of her as Messima's concubine. Things must be up to be invited to Marnon's house.

Exhausted, the companions retired to bed.

***

And now here we are nearing Atlantis Minor thought Messima. She had arranged passage for herself and Néma on a crystal cutter. They had boarded the next day from their semi-private quay beneath the cliffs at the gully just before the exit from the Nile into the South Atlantic Ocean. The crystal cutter was a moderate size with a comfortable private cabin for a couple of passengers. The crossing was uneventful and storm-free in the warmth of early autumn.

Messima thought she recognised Marnon standing on the quay-side. He had always been sensitive to her thoughts and must have picked up on her approach.

The crystal cutter *Nemesis* with its beautiful gilded figurehead of two dolphins and Poseidon's trident edged into the quayside. Its crystal mast with the equilateral cross on a circle symbol emblazoned upon a giant flag in the centre of the ship contrasted against the dark mahogany of the wooden planking. Its long, sleek lines and relatively low draft allowed it to operate in both shallow estuaries and deep water via a keel that could be lowered down.

Torino, the main port in Atlantis Minor, was also the largest town. Messima's uncle Joslin lived to the south of the city with his wife and son Marnon. Marnon, like his father, was a Crystalmancer.

Crystalmancers were specialist geologists who dowsed and searched for the best seams of crystal formations deep under the ground. Atlantis Minor had abundant deposits of large quartz and amethyst crystals deep beneath the crust as well as more accessible seams sloping up towards the surface. The shallow seams once mined out acted as the conduits to access the deeper deposits. It was near one such conduit that Joslin's family lived.

From the quayside, Marnon waved to Messima. She responded by waving back and moving towards the ship's gangway. As soon as the crystal cutter docked Marnon rushed up the stairway to greet the Priestess and her concubine.

Marnon was about the same age as Messima and shared the same hazel-brown eyes and blonde hair as his cousin. Since their fathers were twin brothers, Messima and Marnon could easily have passed for brother and sister.

During the many summers of childhood that the cousins spent together either on the plains of Atlantis or in the wilderness of Atlantis Minor, the two of them were often mistaken for siblings by passers-by or by visitors to their respective parents.

When Messima had decided to join the priesthood, Marnon had tried his best to dissuade her. When she had taken Néma as her concubine, Marnon had been so shocked that the cousins had barely spoken in the seven years since.

Now, as Messima and Marnon embraced, it seemed as if they had never been apart. Even Néma was given a warm hug - much to her surprise and shock. Marnon lifted the Priestess' backpack and hoisted it onto his back.

"Come, it is such a lovely day. I thought we could all walk back and get reacquainted on route to the house."

"Tell me, what is this all about Mar?"

The Crystalmancer paused, opened his mouth, then closed it again without saying anything more.

It was once the Cousins were out of earshot away from the port that Marnon spoke again.

"Things have been happening Mes. Bad things. We feel it in the crystals. A darkness is rising. You must feel it too."

Messima nodded. She had felt a disquiet in her meditations with the crystal arrays over the last few weeks. Some of her healings had failed or needed to be redone when before they had always succeeded. It was as if the harmony of Atlantis was going out of tune.

"I think it's the visitors."

"But surely they have been so kind to us?"

"Too kind," replied Marnon.

The visitors had arrived unannounced one day at the Capital Atlán. They called themselves 'The Watchers' and had brought gifts for the administrative council, including a mechanical man. Reptilian in appearance they had approached the assembly with the story that they were descendants of the great lizards who once roamed the whole Earth but had left after a great disaster. They had watched as humans had blossomed into the civilisation of the great age of Atlantis. Now they were ready to embark upon even better periods alongside them. The council had been enthralled, but the Priesthood had been more cautious in their praises.

The visitors had claimed to be the gods of old – but in the stories, the gods had always glowed with joy and love, and yet the visitors did not. The visitors said it was because humans were now too sophisticated to be held in awe, so they now appeared as equals amongst us. It seemed to make sense. And yet…

"Two months ago, on the eve of the arrival of the visitors, dad had a vision. He saw the destruction of Atlantis. He saw a terrible disturbance in the Earth. The heavens fell. The waters rose and washed everything away. The ice came and covered Torino. When he awoke, he had a terrible fever. I believe that Unc was first taken sick the same day."

Messima nodded.

As the Cousins chatted, Néma daydreamed. She had never been to 'Minor but had heard so much about it from Messima. She could see the mountains in the distance, the dusky autumnal sunlight bathing the red sandstone in gold. The pyramidal shape of the main temple marked the southern extreme of the settlement and their final destination next to the crystal mine.

Néma suddenly felt a tightening of her hand as Messima squeezed it in a sudden panic as two strangers looked at them. The strangers were the visitors or 'The Watchers' as they called themselves. It was the first time that the two women had seen them in the flesh. It obviously wasn't a pleasant experience for Messima, as she passed out.

An hour later, the Priestess woke up on a reclining chair in her uncle's house.

"You had us worried back there Mes," said Néma. "Take it easy, and I will fetch you some tea."

"Let me" interjected Marnon.

Néma sat back down on the seat between Messima and Messima's aunt Augustine. Augustine and Néma had been discussing art and admiring Joslin's portfolio. The latest addition was a complete contrast to the bright and airy paintings of nature. It was a disturbing dark image of a figure standing in a state of heightened anguish.

"Dad painted it that night after his nightmare. He calls it 'the onset of night'. It gives me the creeps."

Everyone sat silently looking at the painting. Messima started coughing.

"I'll get you that tea." Marnon disappeared and reappeared shortly afterwards with a cut crystal beaker of tea.

"Thanks," gasped the Priestess as she took a gulp of the camomile tea.

In the colonies of Atlantis, the absence of hot spring water meant that solar boilers or crystal heaters were used for heating water. The water here was extracted from boreholes in amongst the crystal seams. The refreshing water seemed energetically charged. It certainly revived Messima who got up and moved closer to her aunt.

"How are you feeling Mes?" Chorused Néma and Marnon unintentionally in Unison.

"Better," she replied.

"You are not the only one to faint near The Watchers. Our priests have recorded the same reaction. What did you feel just before you passed out?" asked Marnon.

"Despair, desolation and dread. I'd locked eyes with one of those guys and saw just darkness."

"Our new friends appear to have some secret dark side to their public generosity. They are offering to train Atlanteans in their ways. I can't think it's a good thing." spoke Marnon.

Just as the group was starting to speculate about The Watchers.

Joslin appeared from his room. "Butterfly. How marvellous. And you must be Néma. I'll call you 'Moth'. You can't have a better companion than our little Butterfly."

Both Messima and Néma had flushed with embarrassment.

"Pop, you are embarrassing them. They are not little kids." Exclaimed Marnon.

Augustine chuckled and went out to the kitchen, leaving her husband to settle down in his seat to become the centre of attention as usual.

Joslin was a sixty-year-old sprightly man with wild overflowing blond-white hair. Unlike most Atlanteans, he dressed in colourful striped gowns. Today he wore purple and green stripes brought tightly into his middle with a large black belt. He looked around him as he made himself comfortable in his seat. He had finally settled, putting his feet up on a small stool as he took the juniper tea that his wife had brought him.

"The Watchers. Yes, yes." He said. "Pure evil. I can sense it, and so could my dear departed brother. Their arrival marks the end of the Golden Age and the start of our fall into destruction."

Messima stared at her Uncle. Somehow, she knew he was right, yet at the same time, she was still shocked by his Revelations. Until today she had thought that the arrival of The Watchers meant that humanity would be nurtured into the next step forward. Again, the darkness she had sensed when she had passed the two aliens together with her uncle's revelations cast severe doubts upon that possibility and the open way that the council had embraced the newcomers. Besides, in the legends, the gods of old looked just like us. Yet The Watchers were distinctly reptilian.

Although Messima had never seen an alien before she had communicated with them in her deep meditations. She had found the experience to be very intense but profoundly uplifting. How could her experiences be so different? It was poles apart.

In the duality of existence, darkness balanced the light, and for each benevolent being, there was a malevolent one.

"Messima," The Priestess snapped out of her daydream as her uncle addressed her directly.

"Yes, the truth has dawned on you too. The keeper of the light such as yourself and others like myself in resonance with the earth goddess are in great peril. For the first time in our lives, we must close down our openness to all things and be wary who is connecting to us. The Watchers can sense us and will turn us to their purpose if we let them. Oriel was introduced to The Watchers some weeks ago. The experience I sensed far away here. He was deeply probed for information. It was stuff about you and the priesthood. He closed down the information – kept it away from them - but I think he was harmed in the process. When we both meditated and discussed the event that evening, I could sense a deep dread in his very soul. His deep love for you and his concern for your wellbeing was consuming him. Yes, yes, let's have our supper."

Messima wandered outside with the others. She was relieved to be in the fresh air again. The autumn sun was now low in the sky. Her aunt was ferrying plates of wild tomatoes and bowls of warm wild wheat and barley grains that 'Minor was so famous for onto the large crystal and stone table at the rear of the house. The pale blue render of the dome-roofed dwelling was lit golden with the low sunlight, the shadows casting their shade on the potted dragon trees in the courtyard. The sacred trees appeared timeless – a reminder of the origins of Atlantis and its holy mountain of Olympus.

"Sit." commanded her aunt as she and Néma went off to collect some beakers of warm berry tea.

The meal was a very thoughtful affair. Messima stayed quiet as her uncle recounted tales of his adventures above and below ground in 'Minor. The wild tomatoes and grains were delicious, and she gave silent thanks to the Sun deity and the Earth goddess for their bounty. Néma had unwisely decided to try to match Joslin's and Marnon's wild chilli eating contest. After the third variety, Néma had run to the kitchen to quench her burning throat while the men had descended into raucous laughter. That was one party trick that Messima had given up on a long time ago.

Néma returned a few minutes later looking particularly flushed - some of it with embarrassment. Fresh melons and exotic berry varieties from Europe finished the meal. As darkness fell, they all retired into the sitting room around Joslin's chair.

Joslin checked about him, noting all of those around him, as if for the first time. "Néma, welcome. Any friend of Messima's is a friend of ours."

Marnon briefly glowered at his father before relaxing his features and sighing. "Yes, we must stick together, accept the past and look to safeguarding the future of us all. You, Mes, as a member of The Priesthood, are most in danger. Are the skulls safe?" Messima gulped and said "Yes, of course, in the temple and healing centres. The mind matrix keeps them safe." Joslin spoke now. "The mind matrix will fail - I've seen it. Do not rely upon it. Make provisions."

The Priestess had never for a moment thought of a threat against the crystal skulls. They had been in Atlantis since the start of the Golden Age. They had started the Golden Age with their arrival with the keepers. All thirteen skulls had been retrieved and brought to Atlantis by benevolent aliens centuries ago, carried in procession by exotic looking beings they had been placed in the Great Temple of the Light on the Island of Poseidon. Now the skulls and their replicas resided in the great temple and elsewhere in Atlantis. She was now the keeper of the blue skull known as The Waterman.

When in her possession, the skull or its replica would be placed in the centre of the healing caves to help deepen meditation and aid in different and difficult healing. The assistance of immense knowledge gave the Priesthood, through the skulls, the means to aid Atlantis and its citizens.

The administrative council of the 12 would ask counsel of the 13 Priests of the Cloth – those who wore the aquamarine robes – including Messima. The youngest trainee Priests aided the 13 and tended to the skulls when the main priests were away. Orlin, Messima's senior trainee, was at this moment looking after The Waterman. The skull's true name was only revealed to the Keeper and not spoken outside of the Great Temple. Orlin still didn't know which skull was the replica and which one was the real skull. Very few outside of the 13 even knew that replicas existed. Today the true skull was deep under Medina with her trainee, and the replica skull was in the Great Temple with the others. Messima never travelled when the true skull was utterly alone.

"Are you saying that The Watchers are after the skulls?" asked Messima.

"Yes." Replied Joslin. "They differ from the races described as the Keepers. They may appear to have access to vast knowledge, but their jealousy is just simmering below the surface. They desire knowledge that has been forbidden to them. It is only a matter of time before they act."

"What can we do - if you are correct. The Priests cannot act against the council of the 12." Responded Messima.

"Don't act. Do not let The Watchers suspect. But make plans to safeguard the skulls. If necessary, bring them here to 'Minor. The deep crystal seams that dad and I know of will mask the skulls forever if necessary." Marnon interjected.

"I can't act alone, but I can speak to the others." Messima's tone was firm but calm.

"Please do, Mes," said Marnon.

Joslin changed the topic and spoke of the tales of old passed down to him by the bards he knew in his youth.

Marnon sang and played his lyre. He mainly played soothing Earth songs and melodies. As midnight fell, Joslin took his leave of the others. Marnon showed Messima and Néma to their rooms. Néma shook her head and joined Messima in her room. It would be small but cosy tonight.

Marnon sighed, shook his head and went into his room to sleep. There would be little sleep for the Priestess as she pondered on the conversations from earlier. Néma cuddled her back as quiet fell over the settlement.

X – The Return

Dawn broke over Atlantis Minor. Shortly afterwards, Messima awoke from her shallow sleep and got up. She prepared a peppermint tea and sat down in the lounge next to Joslin's chair. The cold, blue light of early morning together with the onset of autumn made her shiver. She gathered her cloak and cupped her hands around the beaker of tea. As she was staring blankly ahead of her, Marnon appeared.

"Morning Mes."

"Morning" she replied.

"You look tired," remarked Marnon.

"Hardly surprising," she replied. "Let's meditate on the options."

"OK."

The two Cousins sat back to back, bow-legged on the floor holding hands. Breathing deeply, they hummed together until they reached a harmonic resonance. All kinds of images and sounds raced through their minds. Shared memories of those happy childhoods, the accident where Marnon fell out of a tree onto Messima, the joy of her finding an orphaned baby deer in the woods, the campfires around which the extended family would sing. More recent memories surfaced too. The funeral pyre for her father, the encounter with The Watchers, Joslin's revelations, images of the blue crystal skull.

The skull spoke to them both. "I am safe for now. The darkness is not yet strong enough to breach our defences. But the time will come when I will have to leave you. No ages are eternal.

For every light, being is a being of darkness. Those that you call The Watchers - The Annunaki – we know as The Wanderers. Cast adrift from their star system alone with their flight it is hardly surprising that they covert your shining world at its pinnacle of enlightenment. Darkness will fall. But a new light will dawn just as things seem at their darkest. You will both return at that time as will I. I look forward to a long rest beneath the Earth. At a point on the physical realm that you occupy, I will lie deep beneath the ground until I call again. Hidden must my brothers and sisters become also. The Priesthood must also hide - when the time is right. The portents will tell you when."

Images of a comet in the sky and the brightest Aurora filled the cousins' minds. Glimpses of lava flows, vast oceans of water and deep ice sheets were seen as Messima and Marnon returned from her deep meditation. The cousins stood up, and with tears in their eyes, they hugged.

"I must return – The Waterman can not be left alone with my trainee." Said Messima.

"He is safe for now. Why not stay a day or two so that we can plan for his safe passage here when the time is right."

Messima nodded. She felt strangely relaxed now. The way was more certain even if it held much sorrow. She followed Marnon into the kitchen. The two Cousins divided a ripe watermelon into pieces using a razor-sharp obsidian knife and placed them on to glass plates alongside nuts and berries gathered from the woods nearby.

The fresh fruity aromas gave the Priestess a more optimistic outlook on recent events. When Marnon and Messima returned to the lounge, the others were up.

Messima greeted her concubine before smiling at her aunt and uncle.

The breakfast was carried outside into the courtyard. Fresh berries, nuts and a warming vegetable soup along with hummus provided sustenance for the Priestess, her extended family and her companion.

After taking their fill of the fruits on offer Messima and Néma helped to clear up the breakfast things. The porcelain plates were separated from the wooden spoons, forks and obsidian knives before being washed under the cool spring fountain and its perfectly clear and crystal cleaned water.

When all was clean, Marnon started speaking again.

"We should show you the place in the mine with the blue seam. It is at some distance from here. We should go straight away. But you two should travel incognito. I suggested you dress up as a local artisan Mes and you Néma with your short hair dress as a boy. That way they won't be looking out for you."

"What, who?" Asked Messima.

"The Watchers," Marnon replied.

"How many of them are there?"

"Two or maybe more. But they are particularly interested in The Priesthood. And a priestess visiting Minor in early autumn is too tempting for them to ignore. We need to be on our guard." Said Marnon excitedly.

"OK, can we borrow some clothes?"

"Sure., Come this way."

Before long Messima was dressed like a younger version of her Aunt while Néma was disguised in Marnon's old clothes. Néma's hair still needed tying back, so she wore a scarf around her neck to hide it. Messima's hair was braided into a lengthy pigtail then wound around on to her head before being fastened by a hairpin made from local ivory. Elephants we used to aid with heavy tasks in the mines as well as living in herds on 'Minor.

The elephants on 'Minor were closely related to the woolly mammoths that were later found in the arctic regions after the climate changed. These elephant/mammoths had little hair apart from on their heads. They had huge ears and an excellent set of tusks. Many tusks were found quite naturally in the wilderness and were turned in to exquisite items by local artisans. It was appropriate that Messima appeared like a local lady.

"You two look great," said Marnon. "Let's head off in separate groups and take different paths to the mine."

The Priestess nodded.

"Dad will go with you Mes, and I'll take this lad with me. Ow!"

Néma had given Marnon a sharp rap to his ankle. She had a fiery temperament and did not take too kindly to wearing male clothing. The lad jibe was more than she was happy to accept.

"I'm not enjoying this charade, you know. I hope this is necessary." She said brusquely.

"Oh, Ne we need to play along. It's for The Waterman after all." Messima interjected.

Néma sighed and nodded in agreement.

Néma and Marnon left first heading out to the west before doubling back towards the north. Messima and her uncle left a few minutes later taking a more direct route to the east then north. The Watchers did pass Néma's group but showed no interest in them.

Skirting the northern outskirts of town Joslin and the Priestess or rather the artisan passed the wooden shacks of sheep and goat herders and the piles of fleeces being washed before being spun into thread. Acting the part, she stopped at one shack to examine the dyed natural wool as well as the woven carpets produced by a woman of great age sporting one tooth. She beamed a toothless grin at Messima, who smiled back before moving on.

Once outside the settlement fully the rocky escarpment loomed ahead with the entrance to the mine at its base. The road leading up was surrounded by walls encrusted with crystal fragments of all different colours and hues. Messima could feel the energy within the crystal seams and it made her feel breathless.

A large crystal block was being levitated across the road by a man with a copper wand. He lifted his other hand with a happy hello gesture to her Uncle, who had been unusually quiet.

Joslin held his hand up in acknowledgement. The man waved his wand rightwards and down, bringing the amethyst crystal bolder to rest on a pile of others near to a small herd of elephants grazing in the mine's pastures. He came over to join Joslin and Messima.

"Hello, Joslin. Are you bringing us, visitors? Pretty ones at that?"

"Yes. This is my niece – Me....Meldora. She's visiting from the south. She's not seen a crystal mine and is wanting to see the deep blue crystal seams. She's an artist and uses crystals in her work."

"Nice to meet you." Replied the man. He was Dorak, the mine foreman.

"Your son and his mate have just gone in. Small lad. Hope he's old enough."

Joslin looked puzzled then remembered that Néma was dressed as a boy. "He'll be okay. Older than he looks."

Messima chuckled at her uncle's comment.

"I'll take you down myself. The lift responds best to me. The wand is tuned to myself."

Inside the mine, Néma and Marnon were waiting for them. Dorak gestured for them to go to the right and climb on a sturdy wooden platform resting on a ledge above a bottomless pit (or so it appeared).

"Mind your step!"

Once on the platform of the elevator Dorak lifted out a small copper rod from a fastening on an upright piece of wood in the corner. Lifting it, he said several swift incantations in the old Atlantean language. The rod glowed, and as he lifted it, the platform started to rise into the air. Gently gesturing the rod downwards, the lift slowly hovered above the pit before beginning its descent.

The pit now lit up with an impressive show of multiple crystal layers all glowing dimly in their base colours of purple, white and a small amount of blue. Messima found herself gasping at the site as she looked down through a crystal glass window below her feet. She had to dig Néma in the ribs as she had let out a shrill, feminine, note of surprise which had noticeably puzzled Dorak.

They were descending more rapidly now and the air chilled as the lift went more deeply. After what seemed an age, Dorak lifted his arm to slow their descent once more. He gestured a sideways action, and the whole lift platform moved to the side, skimming along amongst the bright blue-turquoise seam of crystals glinting with a subtle glow in their subterranean home.

Bringing them to a stop, Dorak again uttered a short, sharp guttural incantation before placing the rod back in its fastening.

"Here we are, the finest seam of light blue obsidian in the realms of Atlantis. Or it was as it is just about mined out. It's rumoured that Poseidon's sceptre is encrusted with crystals from this seam. Some say the Keepers took blocks of crystal from here to craft the blue Skulls – The Waterman for example. I've never laid eyes on him myself, but I hear he appears crafted to perfection in the finest crystal."

Messima smiled. As she was The Waterman's current keeper, she was familiar with his contours and perfections. She also knew that indeed the replica did have its origin in this very spot. As for the original – well - she was sure that his source was actually far distant as his knowledge was also from much further away. But as for a match that would mask The Waterman's presence, this seam undoubtedly provided the answer if such a solution was required.

"Here. Have this sample to take back with you." The foreman had placed a small crystal chip the size of a little finger into Messima's hand. She took a close look at its colour and clarity before mouthing a quiet "Thank you."

After a brief tour around in which she and Marnon had noted skull-sized ledges and cubby holes in amongst the worked-out seam, it was time to return to the surface. Néma had asked Dorak questions in her best male voice to which Dorak and occasionally Joslin had replied.

On the ascent, Dorak had stepped off the lift platform amongst a quartz seam to load a large crystal boulder.

Skilfully guiding the rock into the centre of the group its multi-tonne weight glistened with energy as it came to rest in the middle of the platform. Dorak again skilfully guided them up on their ascent with his rod and magical chants.

Once safely back on the surface Joslin and the others thanked Dorak for his tour of the mine before taking their leave. Again, the parties separated before heading back.

On the return journey, the afternoon sunshine shone brightly with a little bit of drizzle appearing over the distant mountains. The far-off fishing boats in the bay contrasted against the shining sea.

A crystal cutter made its silent exit from the port, its crystal mast and flag brightly catching the low autumnal sunlight.

A sudden feeling of dread filled Messima but realizing there could be Watchers nearby; she hardened her thoughts to shut out the negative emotions.

Sure enough, around the next corner, she saw the same two Watchers walking along the street on the opposite side.

Messima spied some very bright fabrics in front of a local artisan's stall so stopped to pick up a golden robe.

The Watchers passed by apparently without noticing her presence. After they passed, Messima shook her head and handed back the gown to the artisan. The artisan shrugged his shoulders.

Carrying on more quickly now, Joslin and his niece were soon back at the house. Shortly afterwards, Néma and Marnon returned.

Messima's Aunt brought out some large beakers of jasmine tea for each of the travellers and gestured for them to go out into the courtyard garden. Laid out on a table was a variety of the brightest fresh berries, fruits and locally grown melons.

Taking the opportunity to visit a nearby fisherman Messima's Aunt had spit-roasted a succulent trout and placed it on the table amongst the vegetables and pulses. She had performed the Atlantean death and release prayer over the fish to purify its flesh to be eaten.

Messima helped herself. She usually avoided meat but sensed that the fish was a special treat laid out for them by her Aunt with the appropriate blessing, so she ensured she had a small portion. It tasted delicious. 'Minor was renowned for its varieties of fish, and the rainbow trout was a particularly fine specimen.

When everybody was seated around the table, Marnon spoke. "I think we have a possible place to take The Waterman if the necessity arrives. Dad and I can both levitate the lift up and down the pit to reach the blue seam. Several possible ledges could be used to hide the skull. If we take some lime render or clay down with as we can wall him in behind some of the loose crystals. As crystal miners, we can make the joins appear almost invisible."

"Agreed. But as Keeper, I should take The Waterman down". Replied the Priestess.

"It may be too risky when the time arises if you know exactly where it's hidden, you may reveal this to The Watchers. Better to trust us. " said Marnon.

"OK. But I will bring him here first." She responded.

The late lunch turned into early supper as the extended family made the most of a warm autumnal evening to get reacquainted and to get to know in Néma.

Both of the companions changed back into their regular clothes before continuing with the delectable meal spread. Néma seemed to be relieved to be out of boys' clothes, shaking out her dark bob from its hiding place and retiring to a corner to comb it back into life.

Messima had left her hair braided as she intended to travel back incognito to Atlantis the following day. Néma had agreed to go in disguise but would dress as an artist's assistant – a girl assistant.

That evening the family took turns singing traditional Atlantean songs. Néma, who was from the colonies, sang beautiful ballads of the mermaids and their first encounters with Atlanteans. Marnon was particularly impressed and hugged Néma at the end of her performance. Messima could see that her cousin had accepted her concubine at long last.

Joslin sang the bardic tale of the loss of the Atlantean lands to the sea and the ice. The peoples of the earth had returned to barbarism and had nearly died out. Only those people who had migrated to the temperate lands had survived. Atlanteans were the descendants of the survivors and had gone on to repopulate Atlantis at the start of the golden age. The thirteen skulls had been passed to the Atlanteans, and the ancient wisdom of the cosmos made the people wise.

Messima was in tears by the time that Joslin had finished his tale. Images of the skulls, the temple and the vast plains had flooded into her mind as Joslin sang. She was comforted by Néma who hugged her companion as she fell into a near inconsolable state. All of the negative energies placed on her by the presence of The Watchers were released in a cleansing cry by the Priestess.

When Messima was calm, Néma had taken leave of the Priestess' family and brought her to their room. Undressing her, she helped her to bed before washing herself and joining her there. Gently caressing her companion's shoulders, Néma soothed Messima into sleep.

Tomorrow would be a long day, and everybody should be as refreshed as possible.

XI - The Voyage Home

The next day Messima was up before Néma and joined Marnon and Joslin for breakfast.

A restful sleep had brought a deep sense of clarity to the Priestess. Her hazel-brown eyes appeared clear and bright, her body glowing with an inner light. The worries of recent days had been replaced by hopes for the future and plans to be made to ensure the wellbeing of not only The Waterman but also the other skulls and the whole human race.

She vowed to meditate as soon as she could on board the crystal cutter back to Atlantis and contact the High Priest - the keeper of the master skull – 'The one and all'. It is said that the master skull's sacred name equated to 'the word' of creation in the beginning. The pure quartz crystal skull with an elongated alien head resided in the centre of the great Temple of the Light on Poseidon's island in the centre of Atlán.

Quite simply the master skull was the centre of Atlantean civilisation and culture. Even so, a replica skull was present at the base of the master plinth. Vosoon, the High Priest, would know what to do.

"Mes, I will come along with you to the port." Said Marnon. "I want to see you safely on board. Officially your ship is going non-stop to Atlán, but I have arranged for the Captain to put you both ashore in darkness at the Medina wharf below your tower."

"Thanks, Mar." Replied Messima. "And thank you for the fresh fruits, berries and tomatoes for the journey. The cultivated tomatoes never taste as good as the wild ones from 'Minor."

It was true that despite all the varieties of crops now grown across Atlantis and its colonies, only the tomatoes seemed to become less intense in flavour than its wild counterparts.

Néma and Messima gathered their belongings, straightened their unfamiliar clothing and prepared to leave. Messima embraced her Uncle and her Aunt while Néma thanked Marnon for the family's hospitality. What a good turnaround since their arrival. Embracing a diversity of ideas was always better than conflict and here close to home was proof of that.

Messima whispered, "Néma's got a new boyfriend" when the two were briefly out of hearing. Néma shot daggers at her companion and dug her in the ribs before both of the women collapsed giggling in the hallway.

The two of them tried to recompose themselves when Marnon reappeared to accompany them to the port. He appeared puzzled. "Let's go, you two."

Setting off at a gentle pace, the group were not bothered by The Watchers this time. As the Sun climbed high in the sky, they reached the edge of the port with its pungent smells and exotic fragrances. Spices from Zanzibar and other corners of the known world made their way to this port at the edge of the Atlantean civilisation.

Exotic dried fruits from far off places were stacked next to crates of locally caught spider crabs soon to be loaded on the 'Nemesis'. It was fortuitous that the ship that had brought them had needed repairs here after damage from an earlier crossing. The mighty flag of Atlantis proudly billowed in the light wind over the crystal cutter and its elegant decking. Part of the rudder had been replaced. The tiller now was resplendent with a new coat of lacquer derived from local turtle shells (cast-offs from the many local turtles who visited the bay).

Captain Atlee greeted Marnon – they had been at school together - and chuckled at Messima's artisan clothing.

"How the mighty have fallen, Priestess!" The Captain had a

brief crush on her during their childhood and was known for his cheeky but friendly comments. He was now wedded to the sea and his ship. But he still reserved a familiar twinkle in his eye for his sweetheart that never was.

Marnon gave his cousin and her concubine a hug before taking his leave of them.

"Stay in touch." He said.

"You bet. And look after Joslin. Your dad needs you." She replied.

"A deal." He said before turning around and hurrying down the gangplank - nearly tripping on a case full of crab as he did so. A final, regal wave and he was gone.

A few minutes later and the ship set sail. The two-person crew cast off the ropes as the Captain bellowed instructions while interleaving incantations to the crystal stack in the middle of the vessel.

To Messima the mixture of manual labour by the Captain and crew with commands of intent to the crystals seemed particularly odd. However, to seamen putting their trust in incantations to tie and untie ropes and to control the tiller were just things they would not consider so roping and steering were little different to how they would have been in the days of wind power.

Skilful captains such as Attlee did not use wands for making incantations to control the ship. Their minds were so in tune with their ship's crystals that they didn't need the further tuning that the rods provided.

A little way out from the quayside the *Nemesis* bypassed a small group of fishing boats. The fishermen were raising lobster pots full of spider crabs and other local crustaceans.

A small launch appeared from the outside of the Harbour wall and on deck were the two Watches who Messima had spied before. She lowered herself down to sit on the floor and beckoned for Néma to do the same. Shortly afterwards she felt a mental probe emanating from The Watchers. This she countered with her skills as a priestess, thus ensuring that The Watchers were unaware of her presence. The launch carried on by at the same speed before slowing down to dock at the quayside.

Captain Attlee winked at Messima now sitting down on the deck. He remarked "I'm just not happy with The Watchers. My friend's ship was used to transport a couple of them to a western colony. The crystal stack kept dropping its power at times when The Watchers were on deck. Once it was in the middle of the night. He had not known anything like it. I'll not carry them on this ship."

Evidently, the negative energy that Messima had observed was enough to interrupt crystal generators. She would have to report this back to The Priesthood.

"I have reservations about their intentions I must admit. But if the legislative council have made them welcome, I will not act against them. However I will not embrace them while these doubts persist." Attlee added.

"Bob, Truman, I will escort these ladies below. You keep your eyes on the tiller and look out for storms."

Attlee threw his wand to one of the burly, suntanned men on deck.

"Yessir" came a prompt reply as the man caught the wand and touched it to his brow in a semi salute.

"Ladies - this way," said Attlee gesturing to a hatch in the ships planked decking. The women's belongings had already been stowed in their simple cabin as they passed the doorway. The Captain gestured for them to join him in the galley.

There he offered them some of his honey ambrosia, a kind of week mead, which they gladly accepted. The golden liquid was very refreshing and slightly intoxicating. It was the most potent form of drink that the Priesthood indulged in. Messima's father had always been partial to it, so she had been brought up with its presence. It was considered a luxury and its origins dated back to the 'gods'.

Now sitting opposite to the Priestess and her companion Attlee offered the two women some strawberries, tomatoes and a small dish of hummus. He reached across for some pieces of oat bread and a couple of plates.

"It's best to have some food now as it's set to get stormy later. The autumn gales are starting to rise plus there's a chill in the air. I reckon we'll be in chops before nightfall so supper may be a non-event."

Néma helped herself and stacked a plate of food for her friend. The three of them exchanged small talk before Attlee disappeared to go on deck.

Once he was gone, the two women rinsed their plates and glasses under the sink, giving a cleansing blessing as they did so before leaving the galley for their cabin.

After a trying few days and now with a plan in mind, it was an opportunity for the companions to reaffirm their intimate friendship and to unwind in private.

The storm hit the vessel around midnight. The heaving action of the waves jarred the lovers awake. Despite the protestations of Néma, Messima was determined to see how it was.

One of the crew, Bob, intercepted her just below the deck latch. "No need to panic missy. The Captain has it all under control. We're going to divert to the west and shelter off the coast until the worst of the storm dies down. You'd get soaked on deck in your fine clothes. Our waxed jackets keep us dry in the worst swells. Please stay down here. I can ask the cap'n to knock on your door when things improve."

The Priestess was dishevelled in her hasty rush to dress. She sighed and hesitated before replying. "Yes, please."

Bob nodded and answered with a brief "Right" before heading

up on to the wet deck, a small pool of water coming down the hatch as he did so. Messima considered following him up but thought better of it. Instead, she returned to her cabin and the warmth of Néma's embrace.

Around an hour later as the buffeting had decreased and finally stopped, Attlee tapped at the companions' cabin door. Both of the women hurriedly threw their gowns on before Néma opened the door and gestured the Captain to come in. Attlee's gaze dotted about the cabin before settling his eyes on Messima.

"We're anchoring just north of the bay outside the great river delta until the storm abates. We should be able to set off again at first light. I can give you a knock when we're underway, and breakfast is ready. We have fresh spider crab and plenty of kelp as well as green tea, of course."

Messima nodded in response to the Captain, although her stomach didn't want to contemplate food at that moment. "Yes, pleases."

Attlee left them alone. They returned to bed, tired but reassured.

The rest of the night was uneventful with the companions sleeping soundly.

When Truman knocked on the door of their cabin to announce breakfast, Néma was already up, washed and dressed. She passed Messima her flannel and neatly draped the Priestess' borrowed clothes onto the bunk.

Messima dressed, and the two of them wandered up on deck to where Attlee had assembled a picnic breakfast for them all. The green tea was refreshing but a little cooler than they were used to having. The kelp was quite appealing, but the freshly cooked and prepared spider crab tasted divine.

The travellers took their fill of food while viewing the Amazon rainforest north of what would become Buenos Aires as a mist hung over the thick blanket of trees. The occasional strange animal call reached out to sea as the vessel slowly and quietly voyaged along the coast on its way back up to Atlantis.

Messima called out to The Waterman while deep in meditation. Using a crystal talisman, she was able to connect telepathically with the 'talking head', or crystal skull that represented Pleiadean knowledge opened up to the humans on Earth. Néma watched her companion as she sat in a trance on the cabin bed. A faint blue glow accompanied the Priestess' profound meditations, enveloping her in a pure veil of light.

Although she never took part in her companion's connections to the crystal skull, Néma had occasionally been contacted telepathically by Messima while in a trance.

Messima's features were relaxed and peaceful. Within her meditation, Messima discussed 'The Watchers' and the crystal mine hiding place with The Waterman. He, in turn, told Messima of the last time it had been necessary to hide him. Then the simple people of a peaceful agrarian society left the path of their shaman to return to barbarism as natural disasters had caused their crops to fail in the run-up to a new ice age. Their shaman had taken The Waterman to an inaccessible mountain cave in the Peruvian mountains. The shaman, Apnu, had committed suicide beside the skull. Now part of Apnu's soul resided within The Waterman. Apnu had never spoken directly to Messima before, but now he did so.

"Messima, if the people are straying from their true path, we must be protected. Our knowledge is too dangerous to fall into the hands of these Watchers or those who would do their bidding. We have foreseen possible futures. If the crystal skulls are used for dark purposes, there will be great suffering in the world. The Waterman and his brothers and sisters must be taken far away from the Temples and away from Atlantis. The mine will provide sanctuary for The Waterman, but the others must be scattered to the corners of the globe. An age of enlightenment will dawn again as it did for Atlantis. But a dark age of ignorance and materialism will rise first. You and I will awaken the new dawn. Remember."

As Apnu finished speaking the connection with The Waterman was lost. Terrible images of destruction and strange cities flourished and fell in her mind. The final image of an older woman holding The Waterman in outstretched arms towards a middle-aged woman crystallised in her mind before fading away. "Remember."

Messima then fell into a deep sleep. Néma tucked the Priestess into bed and slid in beside her.

The next morning Atlantis could be seen ahead as the *Nemesis* made its way back to Medina. The sunny stillness of a chilly Atlantean day allowed Néma and Messima to see their homeland with its rich, ruddy cliffs topped with trees and bright white rooftops. Their tower and home, tall, but still small at this distance, reminded the companions of the tasks ahead as their sheltered lives were starting to fade into the mists.

Disembarking at the pier below the cliff - apparently unseen - Messima and Néma made their way back home after giving their thanks to the Captain and crew of the *Nemesis*. The vessel was seen quickly speeding away as the travellers looked back towards the river.

XII - The Priesthood

The next day Messima and Néma took the water ferry from the Medina wharf to Atlán. Again, they were dressed as artisan artists with hoods obscuring their faces. Underneath her outside coat, Messima wore her bright blue cloak as Priestess of the Light and the Water. In her backpack, carefully wrapped in lead foil was The Waterman. He had insisted on coming along as she intended to address the council of The Priesthood.

The ferry was unusually busy, but the two women were able to get some seats together. The crystal stack hummed as the boat got underway again.

The reed beds at the side of the Nile were swaying in the light wind. A pair of grey herons flew up as the ferry went past. The high cliffs around Medina had subsided into the flat plains to the south of the capital. Rows of ripe tomatoes were being harvested in one set of fields, while grapes were being picked in another.

The harvest time was busy for the farmers, their families, friends and neighbours all pitching in to assist with gathering the crops. Cooperation was crucial, and for the next few weeks, the community would be pooling resources to harvest, pack and process the various crops.

Messima was uncharacteristically quiet on this journey. Partly as she was known, and was in a strange garb, but also because of the meeting ahead. She did not know if the skulls or the council of The Priesthood would agree to evacuate the skulls to safety.

At the northern end of the Nile, the concentric circle islets around the central plaza of Atlán were all bridged with wharves beside of them.

The main southern port was full of cutters unloading their various wares. The *Nemesis* was at one berth, loading in olive oil for its return trip to Atlantis Minor. Atlee was on deck, but neither woman waved as neither wanted to draw attention to themselves.

A pair of Watchers was near the pier when the ferry drew in. Thankfully this was not their stop. The boat was very nearly empty as they drew into the penultimate wharf on its journey. This stop was for one of the administrative areas of Atlán, with less inspiring architecture than some parts. Tridents were carved into the White sandstone blocks of the government building nearest the pier, the Atlantean flag fluttering over it on a masthead.

This was not usually their stop since the next wharf was the central plaza with the Temple of the Light and the main Palace on the island of Poseidon. But today they would take the bridge over from this islet since it was known that The Watchers congregated by the plaza wharves.

Néma and Messima disembarked at the wharf, carefully ensuring their footing before heading towards the elegant bridge of orichalcum alloy shining golden in the autumnal sunshine, its filigree patterns and dolphin rail end looking particularly bright today.

At the plaza, the Temple of the Light pyramid looked resplendent over the White marble precinct. Its golden capstone with sun disk rose High above them. The bright white limestone facing rose above the plaza many metres into the air. Just below the capstone and engraved in it was the sacred invocation of the sun god Amun-Ra. It stood out with its bold painted letters in the original Atlantean text.

Usually, Messima would leave Néma to do her chores or visit friends while she went directly to the main temple entrance, but today they stuck together and tagged along behind a group of tourists from the colonies.

They were gasping at the quantities of rock incorporated into the temple structure. The companions followed just behind the group, only separating from it as they passed the side entry to the Priests' Meeting chamber. There Messima dove in with Néma in tow. Checking that the coast was clear, she took off her backpack and her outer garments to reveal her priestly robes.

"I will meet you back here in an hour or so. If I am late just pop back every few minutes until I come out." Messima spoke softly and swiftly before hugging her concubine. "I love you."

Néma flushed in embarrassment. "I know. And I love you too. Good luck with your meeting."

Messima nodded, gave a quick wave and disappeared into the inner room.

Inside the chamber, Arkan greeted Messima. "Greetings anointed one. I am chairing the meeting. We are not following normal formalities as these are not normal times. There are just thirteen of us, and not all of us are Keepers. The skulls have already chosen their guardians to take them into exile. The most widely recognised Keepers will have to stay behind to reassure the ruling council that nothing is awry."

"Greetings Arkan anointed Keeper. I understand."

"Let's go into the skull chamber. Do you have The Waterman? "

"Of course. He asked to be here."

"Then let's make a start." Arkan sounded grave.

Messima placed The Waterman on the appropriate crystal plinth under the dome of the skull chamber.

The quartz plinths of smooth, clear crystal contrasted with the roof and sides of the room with their many colours and structures. Yet despite the different types of crystals, the energy of the gems and the balance of the colours was truly spectacular and beautiful. It was a rainbow of crystals in energetic harmony that complemented the crystal skulls that it housed and formed part of the network of crystal stacks that powered the city.

The Primary node of the pyramid and the city was a giant quartz crystal double point pointing up to the capstone of the pyramid and down to the skull chamber where it was directed at the plinth holding the master skull.

The master skull spoke. "We are of one mind. The Waterman agrees with your summary of the facts Messima. The Annunaki or Watchers have charmed their way into a position of power over the Council. The throne will not act against the Council. Their power is diminished since the days of Poseidon. And if we act alone against The Watchers, we will further alienate the Council against us. We estimate that we have no more than three months before The Watchers have total control of the whole city and will move against us. We intend to replace ourselves with our replicas carefully. As I occupy the primary nodal position, I must remain until last since I can also mimic the actions and counsel of my siblings. Each of you assembled here are to be tasked with escaping with your skull and concealing it until the time is right to come out again in a new age of enlightenment. If The Watchers or their followers do intercept any of us, then the originating race may have to intervene directly. This would be unfortunate. Your skulls all have a separate plan of action in mind for you guardians. A cache of supplies will be sent to all of you nearer the time. You will be given enough wealth to book standard passage to your destinations for yourself and companion if you require to take them. However, we would caution against that unless your companion is proficient in mind blocking against the mind probes used by The Watchers. We will commence the deception one week from now, in ascending order of seniority. Messima and Arkan, you will be in the final wave as you are more likely to be missed. Are there any questions?"

One of the trainee priests put up is hand and started to speak. "Can we return here after we have deposited our skull?"

The Waterman answered him. "No. You must stay hidden at or near to your final destination, with no communication with anybody here. You will have to make a new life away from here. If necessary, you may need to make the ultimate sacrifice. Desperate times call for desperate measures. Though if you make it to the point chosen by your skull, you should be able to settle down with a native population. Your skull will teach you enough words that you can assimilate."

There were a few gasps around the chamber, but a lot of nodding at the end of it. The first two skulls were substituted by their guardian and placed in backpacks for their eventual onward journey. In effect, the last full council of the thirteen skulls had just taken place. Nobody could tell when, where or if there would ever be another one on the planet. Only time would tell.

Messima took a long look around the chamber. So many memories during her years as a priestess. She packed The Waterman in the lead foil and put him in her backpack for the return journey.

When she appeared outside and peered around, she found that Néma had just arrived and was inspecting a flask of wine that she had just purchased in the city. She immediately went up and hugged her companion.

"What was that for?" she asked.

"Oh, just for the time ahead. Nice wine. I think we may need that tonight."

"OK. Temple visit followed by wine the same evening. Strange times indeed."

Messima laughed and took Néma's hand. It was time to go back to the wharf and get the ferry back home once more.

XIII – Flight

S o it was that ten weeks after the council meeting in the great temple that Messima and Néma were packing for their journey into exile. Messima had spent many sessions teaching and testing Néma's ability to hide her thoughts from the mind probes. Now she was adept.

The Watchers suspected that something was going on as there were now citizen's patrols with and without the presence of Watchers to stop and search people suspected of stirring up disorder. And often it was priests who were being monitored or harassed. Even here in Medina, Messima had been challenged by search teams. As she knew many of the people doing the patrols, she was able to talk her way out of the situations. So far, at least.

The cover story was that Messima and Néma were going down to 'Minor for the solstice celebrations. The passage was booked on the *Nemesis* with Captain Attlee once more. Néma thought that they were going there and had even knitted a pair of socks for both Joslin and Marnon. When her exuberant concubine showed Messima them, she smiled and congratulated her companion, but inside she felt sick to her stomach. The plan had changed.

The *Nemesis* had taken on special high energy rations at its normal wharf. Those were destined to be unloaded with the two women at their final destination. Due to new travel restrictions, no unauthorised stops were permitted by ships throughout Atlantis, and all voyages had to be registered and scrutinized. The *Nemesis* with its regular trips to and from 'Minor did not raise any suspicions. Not until now, anyway.

The two women, dressed as artisans with warm cloaks and backpacks, were sat at the Medina pier a few minutes before the rendezvous. It had been a sad time to say goodbye to their tower and all of its memories.

Messima had hugged each of her dolphin friends at the end of the final healing session two days previously. Néma knew that they might not be coming back anytime soon, but didn't know that for sure. Only Messima and The Waterman knew the full plan.

At the appointed time the *Nemesis* appeared in view as the light was fading and veered over slowly to the wharf. The crew hastily lowered down a gangplank, and the two women ran up with their backpacks. As soon as they were aboard the cutter was underway again, veering back into the correct channel.

"Hello, again, ladies. Next stop Peruvia, eh?" Captain Atlee divulged the final destination.

"Peruvia? Don't you mean 'Minor?" Néma asked.

"No, my sweet. The plan has changed. 'Minor is swarming with The Watchers now. It is far too dangerous. We are going somewhere safer. Hopefully."

Néma scowled at Messima and stormed down to the cabin below. She was upset not to have been included in the final plan.

Messima followed her. Néma slammed the door and locked it behind her. Messima tried the door and knocked on it to get a reply. "I am sorry, my love. I couldn't take the risk of you knowing. I know you could stop mind probes, but if they had taken you into custody and drugged you who knows what they might have found out from you. It was for your safety too. But come out my darling, as I have a fantastic surprise for you. It's shiny."

"Shiny? How shiny?"

"Very."

Néma unlocked the door and came out. The tears had made her eyeliner run down her face. She wiped her cheeks and dried her tears.

Messima got down on one knee and passed Néma a small box. "I have now officially left The Priesthood, so my vow not to marry is null and void. So, will you marry me?"

"It's beautiful." Néma examined the ring that Messima had given to her. It was a thin gold band with a dolphin motif and emeralds together with amethyst gems set around it. Néma tried it on. It fitted perfectly. "Yes, I will marry you. But no more lies. Ever."

"I promise my darling. Shall we ask Captain Attlee to do us the honour?"

"OK, then. But won't your family be upset?"

"I don't think so. And we may well never see them again either. I hinted at that on my last meditation with Marnon. He suspects we have moved to plan 'B', I am sure."

Captain Atlee was only too willing to oblige. His teenage crush was never going to be his regardless. He took the simple service and watched as Messima produced a second matching ring for Néma to give to her. At the end, they stood kissing and holding hands for a full two minutes. Captain Attlee was blushing at the end of it.

"Um, congratulations, ladies. We better get on with supper as I am expecting a swell later on as we beat across to the coast where you will be rendezvousing with your onward transport. Darry is a good guy, and I know that he has the skill to get you around the Cape to your destination."

Supper consisted of a delicious spider crab soup with crusty rolls and fresh grapes. Not quite a wedding feast, but indeed a tasty meal.

The love birds retired to their cabin to enjoy their wedding night. The wind up on deck disguised most of their screams, though Bob did wink at the Captain during a lull in the storm when they heard some noises from below.

The next morning the two women were looking a little tired when Captain Attlee brought down a plate of breakfast for them and knocked on their door. Messima had hastily put on her nightgown and collected the tray with a smile. "Thanks, Captain."

"That's OK, Messima. We probably have two hours before we rendezvous with the *Cutlass*."

The women sat down and ate their breakfast together. Afterwards, they washed and dressed, ready for the transfer to the *Cutlass*.

At around noon another ship came into sight. She was bigger than the *Nemesis*, but of a similar design. This was a colonial cutter with two separate crystal stacks and two wooden masts. Messima had never seen one herself as they tended to call at the northern ports on Atlantis. It was prepared for stack failure mid-voyage.

The second ship was indeed the *Cutlass*, and the two crews signalled each other.

After a few minutes of careful manoeuvring, the ships came together, and the men transferred the small items of cargo and the women's luggage onto the *Cutlass*. Captain Darry briefly boarded the *Nemesis* to get his payment and to down a quick drink with his old friend Attlee. He greeted the ladies then hopped back to his ship before helping the two of them onto his boat. They thanked Attlee, then waved to him as he headed back to 'Minor where he would be claiming a partial stack failure caused his late arrival.

Captain Darry welcomed the couple aboard and showed them to their cabin. It was one of four this time, but the others appeared empty.

"Well, ladies, we have a rough voyage ahead. The Cape is unlikely to be too forgiving, so you may need to sit tight for some of the time. The cabin has ship's biscuits and wine in the store cupboard. I trust you can amuse yourselves for long periods below deck?"

Messima and Néma turned to each other and sniggered, while Darry seemed puzzled.

"OK. Supper is at five tonight. Then the next mealtime will depend upon the passage. We will get you over to your destination in about a week. It's pretty bleak up there, but the coastal farmers are friendly enough. One or two of them even have Atlantean wives. You may be in luck."

Néma appeared a little annoyed at that comment, but Messima tried to calm things down. "Thanks, Captain. I guess we will see what occurs. But I don't think we are in a hurry to settle down. We want to explore and maybe teach the locals a few things. We also want to visit the mountains while the weather is in our favour."

"As you wish. I can let you have our best chart of the area. Do you have a compass?"

"Yes, I do. But the chart will be ideal. Thanks."

"My pleasure. You are Harmonie and Wenda I know, but who is who?"

"I am Harmonie piped up Messima. Wenda and I go way back."

"Yes, we do." Added Néma.

"OK. If you need anything, I will be above deck. The galley is two doors down when it's supper time. I am afraid it's nothing special—pickled meat and biscuits. We don't get many passengers. It's mainly metals here. We pick up tin and bring in copper in exchange—occasional gold. I look forward to chatting later. See you then."

The companions practised their cover story and their new names. They also hid their wedding certificates just in case. By five o'clock they had it all straight, plus their matching 'friendship' rings.

The Captain gave plenty of useful information on the area of Peruvia that the women were heading towards.

After the meal, it was very rough for the next two days. The bucket got a fair amount of use by both women, and in quieter periods the lavatory too. The ships biscuits stayed untouched, though the wine did assist. They slept through the worst of it. It was too rough to be amorous, though staying hugging made them feel safer.

The four quieter days they were able to go up on deck and enjoy different pickled meat dishes at mealtimes. The far offshore occasionally came into view to give them a sight of what we today know as Chile and southern Peru.

On the seventh day, they were approaching land and their final destination, the fishing port of Callao as it is known today. There they could hire a guide or buy a donkey for their hike into the mountains. The Captain's chart showed a trading route up into the hills, but it was several days hike away. With the lead foil off of The Waterman, he was able to advise on the best course of action. He suggested that they hire a guide to get to the first mountain town and buy a donkey plus provisions for the journey ahead.

The ship berthed at the port and offloaded the companions on the coast of Peruvia. The Captain said his goodbyes and wished them the best of luck.

At the market, The Waterman was able to telepathically tell Messima the words she needed to hire a guide and to buy a donkey too. A small collapsible yurt style tent was also purchased along with straw mats. At least the journey would be more comfortable.

In reality, the nights may have been bearable, but the hike itself was arduous. The paths were often narrow, slippery or otherwise impassable. The guide helped them cut through one section of forest where a landslide had wiped out the previous track. Thankfully large parts of the trek were well-trodden, and the first mountain settlement was reached after a week. They bid farewell to the guide and carried on towards the point chosen by The Waterman.

After another gruelling week of travelling up and down mountain passes, they reached the fabled mountain.

Here Messima left Néma with the donkey and climbed to the summit. The Waterman indicated a sunken cave to the edge of a screen wall near the summit. Messima jumped into it and was shocked to find a very decayed skeleton next to a ledge with a dark stain where a piece of leather had decomposed. It was presumably the skeleton of the shaman Apnu.

"Here." Said The Waterman. So Messima placed the crystal skull on the shelf, kissed it gently then wrapped it in the goatskin she had purchased at the mountain settlement under the skull's orders.

"Thank you, Messima. You have been a good Keeper. Now go and enjoy a good life down in a nearby valley. There is a matriarchal tribe that would require a healer and a carer such as you and Néma. I will stay awake long enough for you to learn their language and integrate with them. I have told the donkey the route. Now please cover this cave with the loose stones and rubble to hide me. One day, in another lifetime, we may meet again. Goodbye, Priestess."

Tears welled up in Messima's eyes as she left the skull and covered him over with the loose stones and rocks. Soon enough, there was no trace of the cave.

"Goodbye, my friend. Sleep well."

The Waterman was, of course, correct about the tribe. The two women were accepted into the group as healers and allowed to live together in a hut at the edge of the settlement. It wasn't quite Atlantis, but it was now home.

Some months after arriving there was a massively loud sound that came to them from the east. The ground shook for a few minutes before it settled down again. A violent storm waged for the next two days. Messima knew it was the destruction of Atlantis. She wept for her past life, then thanked Amun-Ra for their salvation.

XIV - Anxiety

T he jet ski was long gone as Stan managed to locate and drag Diana's body to the shore.

He rummaged through their things in the beach hut to find his phone.

He was shaking as he rang 911. He feared the worst.

As the rescue helicopter touched down only five minutes later, the paramedics leapt out and shone their torches on the lifeless body of Diana. She felt clammy to the touch, but there was a slight pulse as one nodded to the other to get the stretcher. The senior paramedic attached an oxygen mask over Diana's face and examined her head injury. There was a very deep gash, but the blood flow was a small trickle.

Stan helped them to carry Diana on her stretcher into the helicopter.

As soon as they landed the senior paramedic took the radio and called for a crash team at Miami's Atlantic University Hospital to meet them at the rooftop helipad.

A few minutes later, Stan watched helplessly as the crash team took his bride into the bowels of the hospital while he was ushered to the waiting room.

The interval was agonising. When Stan asked, nobody seemed to know anything. So he sat with his head in his hands, fearing the worst.

Eventually, a doctor appeared.

"Stanislav Havel?"

"Yes. That's me."

"Ah, Mr Havel. Your wife is alive. She is lucky. The glancing blow from a jet ski I believe knocked her out very quickly. That in itself may have minimised damage to her brain. And also probably prevented her from drowning. Your prompt actions certainly saved her life. But she is a very sick young lady. We are keeping her in a coma to protect her brain from further damage. Preliminary scans indicate only superficial swelling. But we cannot be sure until it goes down. She must remain sedated with a feeding tube until further notice. As a seconded staff member, Doctor Garry is covered for all medical costs here. She will be put in a private room with round the clock supervision. We can arrange for you to stay nearby. May I ask, exactly how many months pregnant is your wife?"

"What do you mean, pregnant? Diana never said anything. "

"Oh, OK. She is, of course, a busy lady. There can be superficial bleeding in early pregnancy. We have known several professional women to assume they were having a light period and not realise they were pregnant. When your wife regains consciousness, I will organise scans and gynaecological exams with the appropriate department. Until then, she is under my care. I am Doctor Lynda Beak, neurosurgeon and specialist in neurological traumas. Here is my card. And don't worry, the prognosis is good. We do have some members of the Royal Bahamas Police to speak to you about the incident. They believe they have caught the offenders. Drinking and fast transport do not make a good combination. We have many incidents on the mainland here too."

"Thank you, doctor. I am very grateful. The news will take a while to sink in."

"I am sure. I have instructed the police that this must be a short visit, so get some rest once they are gone. My colleague here has your room key, a map and details of the hospital. Diana is in safe hands."

The police officers were respectful and just requested an initial statement as well as offering their sympathies for Diana's situation. The taller one, detective White left his contact details. He and his colleague were based at the Bahamian High Commission in Miami and were called in on cases like this where a victim had to be evacuated to the US mainland. They offered to arrange a courier to bring Stan's and Diana's passports over to them.

Shortly afterwards Stan was ushered into his private room on the same floor of Diana's hospital ward. By now, it was early morning, and the Sun was starting to come up. He knew he was hungry, but his attention was elsewhere, and his stomach was tight with anxiety. He lay down on the bed in his clothes, but as he was in his beachwear and the air con was on full, he started to shiver before pulling a blanket over himself. He fell into an awkward sleep.

XV - Hope

Aloud knocking on the door broke Stan out of his troubled sleep. He had been having a horrific dream where he had been swimming in the sea and had become surrounded by pirates on motorcycles brandishing chains and medieval scorpions with sharp spikes. He felt powerless.

"Mr Havel. Mr Havel. Can we come in, please?"

"Ah, yes, OK."

Stan got up and wrapped the blanket around his shoulders before opening the door. Standing outside was a hospital orderly and a nurse in his thirties.

"Here are your passports and a change of clothes that the Bahamian police collected for you from your ship."

The orderly handed Stan a small box, then smiled and walked away. The nurse introduced himself.

"Hi, Mr Havel. I am Staff Nurse Alec Stevenson. I am assigned to your wife's care while she is on our ward here. I am glad to say that her condition has stabilised and the doctor wants to proceed with a series of scans. You may wish to accompany her."

"Yes, of course. Thank you. "

Stan quickly opened his package, put on his jumper, pocketed the passports and followed along with the nurse to Diana's ward.

The hospital corridors were dull but well-lit and clean. This was a modern and well-funded teaching hospital.

When they reached the ward, Nurse Alec used his thumbprint to open the sliding door. Once inside, a ward sister looked up and passed over the visitor book to Stan to sign. It was an iPad with a securing cord to the desk. He gave his thumbprint to it and then gave a slight smile to the camera as it prompted him for his photograph. He handed it back to her, and immediately she handed him a printed photo visitor card attached to a lanyard.

Nurse Alec beckoned Stan with him. They entered a private room with a series of monitors wired up to the patient lying in the high-tech hospital bed.

Diana was breathing via a face mask, her injured head carefully sutured and her face otherwise very pale and lifeless. Her hand did twitch very slightly as Stan looked on dumbfounded by the sight of his bride of only a few months in such a dire predicament.

Nurse Alec checked the monitor screens and proceeded to unplug a number of the connections. Once the required amount was disconnected, he continued to lower the backrest of the bed and unlock the travelling wheels.

"Follow me please sir." Said Alec.

Stan obediently followed as Diana was pushed out of her room and along the corridor to an Ultrasound room just outside the ward.

The clinician spoke to Stan. "Are you the father of the foetus?"

"Diana is my wife, and if there is a child, it is mine also."

"Yes, of course. I meant no disrespect. But we have to be careful. Hopefully, your lady will regain consciousness, but if not, you are the legal guardian and have full legal jurisdiction over it. And in the meantime, of course."

"I see."

"I have been asked to do an I initial scan of the womb area to ascertain the stage of the term it has been carried to. You may watch the screen; of course, I will take measurements and determine life functions. "

The clinician wiped and lubed up a stainless-steel probe then applied it to Diana's bare tummy area. The screen showed up a tiny foetal baby with a small head, body and limbs. At critical cross-sections, he paused and used the touch screen to pull down a ruler to measure the size of the tiny creature.

"Your child appears to be in good order, alive and measuring approximately six inches. Which indicates it is around four months in age. I suspect that the gynaecologist will recommend proceeding to term. But they are not bound to my purely indicative opinion. "

"Um, thank you. I am ever more surprised. This is amazing news. I hope she is around for it too." Stan stroked Diana's hand as he spoke. The clinician just nodded.

Alec returned. He tore off a scan, nodded then wheeled Diana back out of the Ultrasound room.

"Follow me, please."

The small party entered a large office at the edge of the gynaecology department. The short south-east Asian doctor looked up.

"I am Hong, Dr Hong. Sit down please."

Dr Hong took the notes and the scan from the nurse. He muttered, then shook his head plus nodded a couple of times as he pulled up Diana's details via the barcoded note sleeve.

As he looked up at Stan, he spoke.

"We will have to see if your wife regains consciousness before the due date or if we have to intervene at the appropriate time. The baby appears to be in good condition and is in its second trimester. The mother appears to be feeding it correctly, but we are at early days after her accident. I have asked to be kept informed at all times for any changes. I am recommending rich feeding tubes be connected to feed both, um, Diana and the child. From the initial tests, it is likely to be a girl since the hormones do not indicate any elevated testosterone in the bodily system. But without further information, intersex or male states are still possible if less likely. Due date is approximately four months hence."

"Thank you, Doctor. It has all come as a shock to me as I didn't know she was pregnant. "

"It could be that she wanted to surprise you, but usually that would be a few weeks earlier in my experience. More likely and increasingly common is 'working woman syndrome' where a busy woman with less regular periods dismisses the possibility of pregnancy when she sees the occasional bleeding she gets from the early stages of carrying a foetus. I see a lot of it. I hope that she regains consciousness in time to enjoy her motherhood. And with minimal damage, of course. Good day to you."

With that, they were on the move again back to where they started.

At the neurological trauma ward, Diana was plugged back into her monitors.

Alec spoke. "We can't do a full-body CT scan due to her pregnancy. But from the initial scan, we are hopeful that the healing process will kick in and minimize the damage from the blow. Despite the bruising and blood you saw, and can still see, she was lucky and the prognosis is good. But there is no guarantee that she will regain consciousness I am afraid. We are now in a waiting game. Can I get you some coffee?"

"Ah, yes, please. Diana is strong. She will pull through. "

Stan stood next to his wife's unconscious body; the tears welling up in his eyes. He clenched his fist and punched the air. "Why, why, Diana? Please come back to me!"

There was not a sound to be heard in the room apart from the pings and hums of the monitors, and yet he suddenly felt comforted as he was convinced that a small voice in his head had said "She will be OK. This is not her time."

Alec returned with the coffee for him.

"Are you coping OK with this, or would you like some counselling? We can provide it for you."

Stan shook his head. "No. I will be fine. I am positive she will pull through."

After his coffee, Stan was so exhausted that he just had to go back to his room for a snooze. He asked Alec to call him if anything changed with Diana's condition.

XVI - Waiting

Stan did manage to sleep for just over four hours.

He dreamt of beautiful sights where Diana was swimming in clear pools of water or standing surrounded by sparkly crystals. It was very comforting and relaxing for him.

Even when he awoke, he was more relaxed than for a long time. Memories of the accident came back, but they seemed less real than the dream, less relevant and much less critical.

When Dr Beak knocked on his door, she was greeted by a more upbeat Stan, freshly showered, changed and even shaved.

"Come in."

"Ah, Dr Havel, your wife is responding well to stimulants. We will have to wait at least a week before all of the swelling has shown itself. But early signs are good. She had a lucky shave with death, I think. Another inch to the middle and things would be much worse."

"I am feeling more positive now. But I will not rest peacefully until Diana is back with me again. "

"If the swelling appears to be superficial in a few days, we will let her come out of her coma naturally. "

"Thank you."

The doctor left the room, and Stan sat back down. He sighed and plugged in his air tube earphones. Now for another hard task. To inform Diana's mother about the accident.

The phone rang for two rings, and Diana's mother answered.

"Hello?"

"Ah, hello, um, Mrs Garry, Karen. I have some bad news."

"Oh, my God! Diana isn't dead, is she? Oh those Americans with their guns, I should have stopped her. Oh, no!" She started crying hysterically.

"No, no, she is alive. But she was involved in an accident. She was swimming when a jet ski came out of nowhere and hit her head. She is injured and in an induced coma in a top hospital in Miami. She is under specialist supervision, and I am with her. The prognosis is good for her recovery, but it is early days as the accident was yesterday evening and the swelling on her brain needs to reduce again before she can be brought round. But I will keep you informed. "

"Oh my God Stanley, I mean Stanislav, I mean Stan. This is all such a shock. Has the jet ski person been arrested? This is awful. This sort of thing you don't expect to happen to your own flesh and blood. That poor Kirsty McColl was run down while swimming in Mexico. She died. Oh, poor Diana. Let me pack and come over."

"I don't know what good that would do but, I entirely understand if you want to. I am sure we can find a hotel for you. We are not that well off to pay for too much though as our wedding cost quite a lot of course."

"Don't worry darling. I will not impose. Diana's daddy will book it all for me. What is the name of the hospital? You must give me the ward details so we can send cards and flowers anyway. My poor dears I will come over straight away. "

Stan gave his mother-in-law all the required contact details. After the customary goodbyes, he turned his phone off and sighed again. Good grief, he thought. I am sure I could do without her mother around us 24/7. He sat down and made himself another coffee then started another call.

"Hello, my darling sister. How are you? And how is your beau, Tara?"

"Super dearest brother. We have some wonderful news for you!"

"Well, I have some more distressing news first, I am afraid. Diana is in an induced coma after being hit by a jet ski last night. It has been the most awful experience of my life. The doctor said she should be OK in the end, but..."

The tears welled up and were let loose as he sobbed uncontrollably on the end of his phone. The tears rolled down, and he was inconsolable.

"Oh, you poor boy. That is awful. Tara, my lovely, Tara, come here – bad news."

The sound was muffled as Stan's sister first called out to her partner, and Diana's sister, to come to the phone. Stan heard more muffled voices followed by a shriek as Tara got the news. When things had settled, it was Tara on the line.

"Stan, how is she now? Will she be OK? Is she going to come round soon?"

"Hi, Tara. Wish we were chatting in better circumstances. Diana is in an induced coma. She had a big gash on her head from the jet ski, and it has bruised her brain. Until the swelling goes down, we won't know if there is permanent damage. It is a waiting game. Your mother may well be on her way here. You could try stopping her if you want, but I don't think it will make any difference. "

"Thanks, Stan. As you know, we are a force of nature in the Garry family. Mummy will take herself over to you, and fingers crossed, Diana will pull through like the fighter she is. She survived the fall when she was a kid. She will do it now. Besides, we want her as our bridesmaid. And you as our best man. "

"What? Are you guys getting married? That is fantastic. I wish I could tell Diana the good news. I better tell you our other surprise. We are going to be parents. Most probably of a girl. But that last bit of information can you please keep to your selves."

"Oh, wow. How many months?"

"Around four. So, July or August, maybe?"

"Awesome. When Diana is back from her forced rest, we will have to organise a baby shower for her. And we may need to look at wrap style bridesmaid dresses to accommodate her bump, or what remains of it as we are having an early September wedding. Daddy's managed to wangle the use of Corfe Castle for the wedding and reception. OK, it will be in a tent mostly, but it's home. We are going to be living in Swanage. Your sister is a natty diver and fisherwoman, so she's going to be running diving and fishing tours around Poole Harbour and the coast here."

"Wow. Congratulations. We all have a lot to take in."

"Very true. You get that sister of mine well again, Stanislav. We are all counting on you."

"I will do what I can. But most of it is down to the medical care here and Diana herself."

The couple swapped over so Stan could congratulate his sister. Then they agreed they would receive updates when anything changed. As Tara was generally broke and was saving up for her wedding, it wasn't an option for her to come over. But she would be there in spirit. Tara would pass on the news to their other sister Aphrodite.

Stan put the phone down, then lay back down to rest and sleep.

XVII - Visitors

"**S**tanley-slav!"

Karen Garry called out to her son-in-law at the arrivals gate. She had (partially) corrected herself as she called out his name.

"So glad to see you. How are you, and how is my sweet daughter currently?"

As she spoke, she held out the handle of her largest case to Stan.

"Uh, okay thanks, considering. The dig has given me a leave of absence. Diana is still sedated. The swelling has peaked and is now going down. Tomorrow they will do the main scan to see what damage is in situ. That will determine if she can come out of sedation or stay under longer. It is a critical day. I doubt that I will sleep tonight. "

"I see. We best head over. Thank you for organising a guest apartment for me at the hospital. "

"They have been outstanding. It is a staff benefit. There is a shuttle bus about to go there, leaving in two minutes if we can just get to the door now."

"Of course. The sooner, the better."

The relatively short journey from Miami International Airport to the hospital was filled with Mrs Garry telling Stan about all of Diana's relatives – most of whom Stan had either never met or only extremely briefly at their wedding the year before. He was too fatigued after days in the hospital beside Diana or collapsed in his room to offer much in the way of conversation. His mother-in-law barely noticed.

Once back at the hospital, she was scanned into the facility and given her visitor pass and combined room key.

Nurse Alec ushered them both up to see Doctor Beak.

As they entered, the doctor looked up and smiled.

"Good news. We were able to take Dr Garry up to the CT scanner and get a full scan. I appreciate your reticence to use x-rays, but it is sometimes necessary. Our equipment emits approximately $1/20^{th}$ of the dose of a similar machine from only five years ago."

She continued as Stan frowned slightly.

"The results are incredibly positive. She has only superficial swelling on the surface of her brain. No signs of any internal or external bleeding. The prognosis is excellent. We can allow her to naturally awake from her coma if you are agreeable. "

Stan thought about complaining about the unauthorized scan but thought better of it. What is done is done.

"Yes, of course. When is she liable to wake up?"

"By suspending sedation, she should be awake early tomorrow morning, all being well. "

"That is fantastic news. Will she be lucid?"

"We will see. That is the big question, of course. "

Stan signed the required forms on the iPad, then was whisked out of the office.

"I will be in touch. Diana should probably be left to rest while she is waking up. Go and have a good evening meal and sleep. Tomorrow will be a big day and could start early. I recommend the rooftop restaurant. There is a 50 per cent staff discount running tonight. I would certainly recommend the ribs and the T-bone steak as excellent. The weather is perfect at the moment, and you can get a view over to the Bahamas on an evening such as this."

"Thank you. That is a great idea. Karen, shall we?"

"Yes, of course. I haven't had a T-bone since the mad cow scare back in the 80s. I almost wonder what it tastes like? The aeroplane food was somewhat lacking. With the exchange rate as it is, I had to come economy. The seats were ghastly. "

The pair took the elevator to the roof, then followed the signs to the restaurant. Stan showed his staff card, and to his surprise, they were given a fantastic table that had supposedly been reserved. The waiter winked at Stan as he took the reservation tag off of it.

The view was glorious. A cloudless sky with very little mist revealed a wide vista over the harbour and towards the wider Caribbean. Seeing the Bahamas would be a tall order, though. Key West was just about visible in the distance.

The waiter brought out an extensive menu, plus a bottle of red wine and two glasses 'on the house'.

A lot of kindness had been shown towards him ever since Diana's accident. A lot of people were fans of hers and were very sorry about what had happened. The University and its hospital staff were aware of what had occurred. To make things worse, the jet ski riders had turned out to be Bahamian youngsters who were attending the University as sports delegates. They were great at American football but were academically weak - also renowned for their drinking and drug exploits. Some within the University had turned a blind eye to their antics and were now terrified that Diana or her relatives would be starting litigation against themselves.

In practice, Diana had better things to do than spend years in court, as long as she recovered, of course. The students had been suspended and were currently on bail in the Bahamas without their passports.

Stan had a real craving for some Cajun chicken or swordfish, so was relieved to see it on the menu. A slight tear formed in his eyes as he remembered the romantic candlelit meal, he had shared on honeymoon with Diana just a few months earlier, where he had last tasted the spicy dish. The Caribbean music, the mojito, the atmosphere and of course, her company. And next time will be the same he told himself.

"Oh, beef Wellington. I have not had that since my wedding. How delightful. These Yanks think of everything. What are you having, uh, Stanislav?"

"Call me Stan, Karen. I am going to have Cajun chicken salad with fries. That is, with narrow potato chips."

"Oh, I love the cultural and linguistic differences between the British and our American cousins. I was completely lost out here when I was here for a year with Diana's father while on secondment to a dig in Utah. Thankfully it was before we had the girls. In fact, we might have stayed if I hadn't fallen pregnant. Oh, those cosy nights in the desert!"

Stan smiled awkwardly. His attention wandered back to the vista of the sea, the clouds drifting across the blue sky, disappearing far into the distance. An aircraft sped along against the direction of the wind. As he followed it, a slight movement caught his eye. It appeared to be a large pod of dolphins quite close into shore. Their majestic bodies were glistening in the failing evening sunlight as they jumped in and out while pursuing a shoal of fish. It was glorious, yet unusual here, almost like a special good luck salute to himself and Diana of course.

The waiter came over to take the order. He asked after Diana's condition. Stan gave a quick synopsis, then made the order. They were both going to have clams in white wine followed by Cajun chicken for him and beef Wellington for his mother in law.

Stan was trying not to get too caught up in her tales about Diana's sisters and their various boyfriends. Oddly, she never mentioned any of Tara's girlfriends, but she must know about them. This woman was desperate for grandchildren. Hopefully,

Diana would bring her the joy she craved if she regains consciousness.

The waiter returned with their starters. The clams were sizzling in their shells, the white wine sauce bubbling up to lap at their sides. The side order of ciabatta would be well suited to mop up the pungently aromatic sauce.

The clams were tender yet firm, popping out of their shells easily with the little fork supplied. Even Karen appeared to be enjoying them as she had fallen unusually quiet.

As Stan enjoyed the silence, he imagined that Diana was here with them. A little voice spoke to him in his mind and said 'Don't worry my son, your beloved Diana will be back soon. She needed to listen to her inner truth and memories unhindered. Forgive us for the brutal means. You both should meditate more to attain Kenshō. Enlightenment. '

"Another glass, dear boy?"

Karen snapped him out of his daydream. Or was it a message from his spirit guide? He shook his head slightly.

"Yes, please. It is lovely food. And the wine is not bad either. "

He was surprised to see that his plate was now full of empty shells. He had no conscious memory of eating them all. Curious. The waiter smiled as he scooped up the plate and whisked it away.

The Cajun chicken duly arrived, again sizzling on the plate, the fries coated in Cajun seasoning alongside the blackened chicken breast. French beans filled the remaining space. His dining companion now had a large pastry case on her plate, with dark gravy around it. Her vegetables were on a separate platter. Stan hoped that she had a good appetite. Certainly better than Diana's generally was. That dish would last her for several days.

Much to his amazement his mother-in-law not only polished off her beef Wellington but was flicking through the dessert menu too.

"The sea air always gives me an appetite. I love a big fish and chips along the seafront back home. But I really fancy the waffles right now. How about you?"

"I am good thanks. Just a cappuccino with nut milk will suit me. Not too much caffeine. "

Karen waved at the waiter, who duly came over to take their order.

Stan finished his Cajun dish but left some of the fries. It was bittersweet eating that dish without his sweetheart with him. Soon, he thought. Soon.

The coffee and waffles both went down smoothly. Stan was still amazed by the appetite of this relatively trim lady in her early 60s. How did she eat so much without getting enormous?

The meal done, he paid up and gave the waiter a moderately generous tip. The man lightly squeezed his shoulder as a sign of solidarity. "Good luck tomorrow you guys." His accent was more Brooklyn than Floridian. Obviously an interesting story there too.

They left the rooftop just as the last ray of sun disappeared on the horizon. It was time to go back to their rooms and await the morning with its hopes and aspirations.

"Good night" he heard himself say to Diana's mother as he went into his room on the left with hers on his right.

XVIII - Morning

Stan awoke with a start. A room phone was ringing near to him. He grabbed the handset to answer it. "Hello."

"Ah, Mr Havel. Your wife is starting to come out of the coma. You will probably want to come to her room now. Get dressed first. It will be a few minutes before she is out of it."

"Thank you. I will come very shortly. "

He hurriedly washed and dressed in the clothes nearest to him, then left his room to head to Diana's room on the ward.

At her bedside Nurse Alec was there adjusting the tubes still attached to Diana's arm and around her face.

"Hello, Mr Havel. This is a precaution as all patients coming out of a coma are disorientated, and often they tug at the tubes or try and get up straight away. So standard protocol here is to make them less intrusive and to loosen them, so they don't get ripped out. Diana is stirring. I saw her eyes flicker a short while ago. We should know soon."

In Diana's head, a voice was saying "You must go back now. We have revealed all that you can know at this time. Find those of Cuba who saw the city far below. Give the information to the benefactor directly. Your director can not be fully trusted. He did the easy thing before. Go back now. Leave Messima in her story and return to the ones that love you, Diana. Goodbye."

Diana opened her eyes. The bright lights were a blur. Was she in the tunnel to heaven? The focus started to return—a person in green scrubs above her. Not an angel it seems. Another figure. A familiar person with a small beard. Stan!

Diana let go a gasp. "Stan! What wonders I have seen. It was beautiful. Where am I?"

Diana's statement somewhat dumbfounded Stan. He wasn't expecting it. He didn't know what he had expected. Just not that.

"My darling. I'm here. You are safe now, my love. You are in hospital. There was an accident. I thought I'd lost you. How are you feeling?"

"Actually, I have a numb feeling at the top left of my head. Am I injured? My forehead seems a bit stiff like I've got a bandage on it. What happened? We were on the beach. We saw the sunset. I was swimming. It was getting dark. Then there was a loud noise. A sudden pain. Oh. Was I hit?"

"Yes. Some jet skiers zoomed in on us. One hit you. A glancing blow. But you were unconscious and were brought here by helicopter to Miami. You looked a mess. I was so worried. "

"Miami? And is that...Mummy?"

Diana's mother had joined them by this stage and was smiling down on her daughter.

"Oh, darling. So glad to have you back with us. You had us so worried!" She stressed the 'so' as she spoke.

"What are you doing here? What have you done with Chow-Chow?"

"She is with Aunty Nelly. You know how she hates commercial kennels. I explained the circumstances and Nelly offered. Chow-Chow did pine. You know these Tibetan Spaniels!"

"It's lovely to see you, Mummy. And my darling Stan. But I have had a fantastic dream. At least I think it was a dream. Can I have some paper, please? I want to make some notes and some drawings. "

"You should be resting. Can't it wait?" Stan looked at his wife with concern as he spoke.

"I don't think it will do. I am feeling OK. This drip thing should still let me write in a notebook or something. How long was I out for?"

"Six and a half days. You were brought straight here. You are a lucky lady. We were able to act quickly." Alec piped up as Stan hesitated and seemed genuinely confused by how long they had been there.

"Well then, I am sure I can do a little doodling. I don't feel tired, I can feel all of my limbs, and I know my birthday. 31st December. Will that be OK, uh, Doctor?" Diana turned her head a little to look at the nurse.

"I am Staff Nurse Alec. The Doctor will be here shortly. But subject to her agreement, I do not see why not. I can find you a note pad and pens."

"Thank you, Nurse Alec. Can I ask, do I have stitches in my head?"

"Yes. Just a minimal number amongst your hairline. They should all dissolve in good time. We shaved a small patch of hair, but it should not notice and will grow back."

"That explains a lot. But thank you."

Just then, Doctor Beak Arrived. She gave a brief smile, then checked the patient notes.

"Ahh, Doctor Garry. You have had a remarkable escape. An inch either way and I doubt we would be speaking now. You may make some notes, as I heard your request. But no getting up and no solid food quite yet. You have been unconscious for some time, and your body needs to recover. Please take it easy and let us care for you."

"I will do so. I do feel thirsty. Could I have some tea, please? Or is water better?"

"Water today. Then we will see. You English and your tea!" She chuckled.

After a few more checks and a private chat between themselves, the medics both left the family together.

Alec returned shortly after with a note pad and some pens. He handed them carefully to Diana, who started drawing and writing straight away.

"No more than an hour please Diana. We don't want you overexerting yourself at this stage. I will be back around that time. If you need me sooner or at any other time, please pull the cord." With that, he left the room.

"It really was beautiful, you know," Diana remarked to the room in general.

"I have heard that near-death experiences can be profound and sometimes beautiful. "

Diana chuckled. "Atlantis, my dear husband. I was not travelling down a tunnel of light. I was shown a whole lifetime in the far distant past. Or otherwise, the dream was incredibly detailed. I am writing down key points so that I can write them up later. There are verifiable parts of my adventure. Oh, and we may need to travel to Cuba or track down some Cubans. They discovered part of Atlantis on the sea bed. It was reported but dismissed around the time. I have reason to believe it is real."

Stan and Karen looked at each other, somewhat dumbstruck again.

"You had a major blow to the head. You can't know these things for certain. It is more likely your imagination, surely." Said Stan.

"Maybe, or maybe not. That's why I want to check those verifiable facts. Perhaps you can search online for information on this Cuban deep-water scan of the sea bed that found something. Maybe buildings or a temple complex or an underwater pyramid. If you can find names, maybe we can meet them and find out more. But this is not for the Director. This quest is for our unnamed benefactor. Mr Dusk, I suspect. The Director may have been involved in a cover-up. Perhaps that information is online too?"

"Oh darling, you should be resting, not working or worrying. You are so much like your father!"

"Mummy. I am OK. Well, maybe not OK. But I am well enough for this. I have to write this down, then I can and will rest. I wish I could draw better. These line drawings don't do the real thing justice. "

Both Stan and Diana's mother sighed in unison. They knew that a determined Diana was unstoppable.

"I love you, Diana. You terrified me. You are back now. And as infuriating as ever!"

"Always my darling. I love you for all time. And I promise to be infuriating too."

Stan chuckled and leant over to plant a kiss gently on her cheek.

XIX - Revelations

Nurse Alec returned later on and smiled at Diana until she sighed and put her pad of paper down.

"I know. I am stopping now. I will rest. I promise." She ended with a little smile before moving her head slightly to look at Stan.

"Here Stan. I need you to track down those Cubans who found something under the sea. I think it was back in the early 2000s? I feel it's very important. We may need to contact our benefactor as that would not be part of the dig's remit."

"OK. I will get onto it now. But you must rest and not worry."

"I know my love. Don't fret. I am not going anywhere. But I must say, now that I am not concentrating and the drugs have worn off a bit, I am getting an odd sensation in my tummy. It felt like a kick if that makes any sense?"

Stan and Alec looked at each other. Alec smiled and said "Your call Dr Havel."

Stan looked at Diana and smiled at her slightly awkwardly. "This may seem a little odd, and the wrong way around, but you are pregnant. We are expecting a special delivery in the Summer."

Diana's jaw opened as wide as it was able to with the wires around her.

"OMG. That explains so much. About four months?" Stan nodded. "That explains the irregular periods and spotting I was getting. I am such a fool. How could I not realise? I have laughed at women who have gone to full term without knowing. And now

I have gone and done it. It explains my weight gain, weird tastes on my tongue, and what I can now call cravings."

"Congratulations dear. May I let the family know when I update them on your progress?" Diana's mother spoke after being uncharacteristically quiet for quite some time.

"I guess so. Well, that's something I hadn't thought about if I'm honest—new territory for me. You will get to be a granny at last. Am I your best and favourite daughter ever?"

"Not quite. You gave me an awful fright. You get fully well first, darling."

"OK, that's a deal. I will let you share all of the news."

XX – Miami

Diana regained her strength as the days went by. After another week she was moved to a private room on a regular ward overlooking the sea. Barbara replaced Nurse Alec as the primary nurse assigned to Diana's recovery.

Diana continued to write up her experiences while in her coma. Stan had been able to return partly to work on the dig programme, but based in his room in the Miami hospital. He was cataloguing and sorting the photographs of the finds and other metadata associated with it.

One of the new developments was the deployment of an autonomous LIDAR drone to map the surrounding landscape and dig area at low tide. Rupert had trained himself in programming the drone and had become very adept at setting it off on search patterns.

One such pattern had brought back astounding evidence of several building platforms in and around the dig area that disappeared further into the sea. The results were so clear that the Director had informed the benefactor and the benefactor had loaned the dig an autonomous sonar submarine drone to extend the survey into the undersea area. He had made a team available to assist with it.

The presence of a new submarine with sonar capabilities did open up other possibilities that linked in with Diana's dream and her wish to speak to the Cuban survey team.

If the survey area was near enough to the Bahamas and not in Cuban territorial waters, it just might be possible to make use of the sub to confirm or otherwise their claims. Lots of huge ifs.

But Stan knew better than to discount Diana's intuition. The Roman temple finds at Anet were testament to that.

A short while later, after checking in on Diana, Stan set off for the diving school at the edge of the harbour. It was in a less than salubrious set of buildings alongside fishing boats belonging to members of the Cuban community in Miami. But Stan had been assured that at least one diver had been involved in that survey mission in the early 2000s.

As he got out of his Uber at the buildings, he was challenged by a sturdy, highly tanned man with skin like leather, in fast spoken Spanish. It wasn't Stan's most fluent language, but he knew enough to get by. He replied to the challenge that he was looking for a diver named Pedro Ramirez. Not far off John Doe or Peter Smith in English. Most probably an alias.

"Si. Over there, Gringo." The sturdy man pointed towards the middle building at the edge of the dock.

Stan thanked the man in Spanish. The man half scowled, and half smiled back at him.

The Archaeologist was not accustomed to Miami or local customs, so just headed over towards the building. Thankfully there were no further challenges on the way.

At the building, a couple of divers were cleaning and checking their gear. One of them looked up at Stan as he approached.

Stan spoke. "Pedro Ramirez?".

One man nodded. "Si."

"Great. I am Stan Havel. I have been looking for you. Remember a survey you did off Cuba in the early 2000s. Does that ring any bells?"

"Maybe."

"We might be making a return visit, but we need to convince our backer of its value. If he bites, there will be jobs in it. And we are not talking fishing. I am an Archaeologist, not a treasure hunter or a journalist. What do you say?"

"You are in luck Archaeologist. The surveyors are in town. Go to Hotel Magnifico downtown. Ask for Javiera And Alberto. I believe they may even have some sonar scans plus GPS coordinates. We come as a team. Here's my cell phone number. Call me when you have a plan."

"OK, thanks, I will do. "

With that, the meeting was over. The diver returned to oiling his wetsuit while Stan called up an Uber to take him downtown.

The car arrived quite quickly, though the driver seemed a little bit nervous to be so near this part of the docks. Stan waved to him, and he pulled the small Toyota beside Stan's feet.

"Hotel Magnifico?"

Stan replied "Yes."

The man chuckled as Stan sat down. "There's nothing magnifico about that hotel if you ask me."

Stan smiled back at the man via the driver's mirror.

"It's OK. I am just meeting some friends. I am not staying there. "

The car smelt musky with a touch of sweat. The driver obviously spent a lot of time in it. The seat was comfortable, and the journey wasn't too long.

Once Stan had stepped out of the car, the driver tipped his head to his passenger and sped away. He didn't seem too keen to spend time around there. As Stan looked around, it wasn't hard to see why. A thin, scantily clad woman was eyeing him up from the street corner across the road. From her demeanour and heavy makeup, she spent a lot of time walking the streets. Stan shook his head and went to go in through the hotel doorway. As he did so, a car drew up alongside the woman. A few words were exchanged between her and the male driver before she got into the front of the car with him.

Once inside the lobby, Stan found himself in front of a grubby reception desk. The counter was covered in a broken sheet of black PVC linoleum. The key racks behind the desk were falling down, having been previously tied back on with wire ties.

A scruffy man with a beard and an eye patch was sucking upon a lolly stick as he whittled on a sharp stick with a rusty lock knife.

Eventually, the man looked up and spoke. "Si?"

Stan mentioned the names he had been given. The man shouted to a woman in an adjoining room. A short exchange of what sounded like Spanish expletives ensued until the woman came out and stood in front of Stan.

"What do you want, English?"

"Czech, actually, but my wife is English. She tasked me with finding you. We are digging for evidence of Atlantis over on South Bimini. But it seems you might have found way more. I was wondering if you might be interested in revisiting your findings. We have access to sonar drones."

"Interesting. But what's in it for us? Dusk approached us years ago. I told him to go into orbit. The Cubans would not allow a western survey vessel so close to its territory. Not without guides at least. Who do you work for?"

"I work for the Atlantic University of Miami. We have some funding for recruiting specialists, but I would need to consult with them."

"Do it. We charge divers rates. 1000 US a day. Each. For the three of us. Four weeks minimum. You supply all the equipment, and we will bring the original sonar scans and GPS coordinates. Don't use a US registered vessel. It won't end well. Take it or leave it, Dr Havel."

Stan gasped as she used his name. "How did you know?"

"We know a lot. It was only a matter of time. Cubans have ears."

"OK. But you say you have the original sonar scans. Don't the Cuban Government have those?"

The woman chuckled. "They think so."

"I will need some time to discuss your terms with my boss."

"I think that Mr Dusk will pay this time."

"Why so sure it's him? I have not seen any official link to him."

"I would be amazed if it's not him. But he won't do anything under his name that is linked to Atlantis or the Bermuda triangle. It's too much woo for his fans. You have one week. We have excursions booked and have to pay our bills for this dump. Here is my card."

She handed Stan a card which he took.

"Goodbye." And with that, she was gone. The scruffy man gestured to the door with his knife.

Stan left. His phone in his hand to get the next Uber.

XXI – Expedition

Somehow, the appeals to the director to expand the survey offshore and into international waters off of Cuba got approved by the benefactor. So, at the beginning of May, Stan found himself part of the crew of an old trawler turned survey vessel on his way to the deep water off of Cuba. With a live satellite link back to base he was able to keep in contact with Diana, who was newly back at work but not ready for such an adventure.

The three Spanish speaking divers were also aboard. Thankfully, the receptionist from the hotel had stayed behind.

Three very techy Americans were loading the autonomous submarine sonar drones onto the deck. These were the latest versions as supplied by the 'anonymous benefactor'. If deployed at the right place, these would be capable of mapping details nearly as clear as the LIDAR drone the dig team had been using on land and shoreline. The results, and the consequences, could be staggering.

Once the food and technology were on-board, the Captain used the loudhailer system to tell the crew that they would be casting off shortly. The American drone guys practically gloated at each other when they realised that their adventure was about to start.

The trawler was well loaded, but not dangerously so. The extra hands outnumbered the crew. The miniature submarine at the stern was chained on securely but was unlikely to be used unless the drones failed. Likewise, the diving equipment stowed by the divers. That was for all eventualities.

The Panamanian registered *Cape Cod Rainbow* set sail around 9 AM, bound for a vague area in the Yucatan channel west of Cuba. The exact coordinates were to be shared by the Spanish speaking contingent once they had received confirmation that their fees had been paid in advance. The payment would only be made once they were onboard. An hour of distrust was evident as the woman used her mobile phone to contact her bank. After a few minutes, she mouthed "Si" to her colleagues, then made her way up to the vessel's bridge with her locked briefcase purported to contain the original sonar surveys and the GPS coordinates.

As they cleared the final breakwater, the vessel veered slightly further to the right than seemed necessary. Stan looked up at the bridge from his deck side vantage point. The Captain, a jolly Frenchman called Pascal Latif, was holding up a DVD case while the woman was seemingly explaining something to him as he nodded. It would appear that the new coordinates had been programmed in by him.

As Miami disappeared behind them, the deep sea swells persuaded Stan that it was time to go inside. One of the drone technicians looked decidedly green. This voyage could be a long and unpleasant journey for him. Stan was well seasoned as a sailor from his days helping his Uncle back in Czechia.

The dark clouds on the horizon looked ominously like a sea squall was going to hit a bit later. Even seasoned Mariners would need to take care in such conditions. Stan hoped that the drones were well secured. At least as it was only May, the hurricane season had not yet started this year.

When Stan reached the galley, the woman was sitting down at the table. She smiled at him and said, "Now we can talk, er, Stanislav?"

Stan nodded. "OK. But call me Stan". He sat down opposite her.

"I am Javiera Cortez-Ramirez."

"Were you in charge of the survey?"

"No. But I was a key member. I was in charge of the sonar array. The other two were our dive team. I was also reserve diver. Together we ensured that the survey was not interrupted. "

"OK. So, I take it that you started off doing a standard survey of the sea bed. Looking for oil and gas reserves, I understand. Did you find any?"

"A little. Enough to satisfy our sponsors. The Cuban government were under severe embargoes at the time. And the threat remains. So, having our own, I mean their own, oil and gas reserves are important. With the instability in Venezuela, their supplies could be cut at any time. The state oil company is intending to place Russian built drilling platforms into place in the next few years. They are doing deep drilling on steep angles to get to the deposits currently. But it is not optimal. Cuba is still reliant on imports."

"So, tell me. When did it start to become a non-standard survey?"

"Well, in very deep water at the edge of Cuban territorial waters and international waters, the sonar was bringing up unusual shapes and rock formations. At first, we thought it was an issue with the array, so we stopped, and the divers checked the equipment. It was clear. No echo from debris or other possible causes of false-positive targets. We restarted, and the regular shapes carried on. Some of the formations were huge. We are talking about the size of the Great Pyramid in Giza and the same forms. But also, regular lines and circles of rocks and gaps in between. From my background in geology, these did not appear natural and differed from the known topography of the area. We were all shaken up by the surveys. The Leader - Fidel Castro would have denounced us if we talked of such things. So, we took copies of the scans and then wiped the official ones in the area of the buildings and streets that we appeared to be seeing. Atlantis or another civilisation, this was proof. In Cuba, such legends are not popular. "

"Wow."

"I know. But in America, such things are quite trendy. Area 51 and Flat Earth are massive. Atlantis not so much. But that could change. With our skills, knowledge and your reputation, this could be a breakthrough. Your backer should be pleased. "

"Yes, quite probably. But the integrity of the dig team is at stake. We need solid proof of what is currently thought of as a myth or legend. We need good quality sonar scans, corroborating survey results and clear underwater photographs or we can't publish any of it. If we could even surface some artefacts, we would be in a new world. Anything less and it might not see the light of day. Our Director is a sceptic. "

"It will be OK, I think. We know where to look. You have the technologies aboard and a wealthy backer. I have passed on the coordinates. We will skim very close to Cuban waters, but enough was in International waters. Your Captain told me we would go straight there and take up station. He said he would tell us when we get there. I don't think it will be long."

Stan nodded thoughtfully. Diana would love to have been here. From what she had told him in her recollections of her vivid dream of Atlantis, there had been substantial buildings there. Some pyramids, civic buildings, towers and stone-built dwellings. It could have sunk very quickly, but it was a very long time ago.

How well preserved might it be? Would its structures now appear like natural underwater cliffs? How precise would the evidence be? This could be an archaeological discovery beyond that of Tutankhamun's tomb. Or it could be career-ending – condemned to the far side with Damon Ice and Al James. He shuddered. It could be a long couple of days ahead, and perhaps he should get some shut-eye.

He took his leave of the Cuban contingent and headed down to his tiny cabin.

$\mathcal{XXII}$ – $\mathcal{D}awn$

It was at first light the next morning when a klaxon sounded to announce their arrival on station. Stan must have been more tired than he realised as he was awoken by the sudden alarm and the clattering of feet and equipment above deck.

As he arrived topside a few minutes later, he saw sonar arrays being deployed from the stern of the ship, plus two UAVs being lowered along the side. The sea swell had thankfully calmed, and the early morning light was starting to show a relatively smooth dark green ocean in front of a bright, sunny sky. A couple of seabirds were circling above the mast, a small shoal of fish jumping off of the port bow. If it were clear enough to see that far Cuba would be on the starboard side as they headed back northwards tracking along the original scan path from the early 2000s.

Realising that he may be missing out on some returning data, he headed up to the crowded bridge. There the UAV geeks were cheek-by-jowl with the sonar operators. A mixture of Spanish and American expletives broke the air as the first responses came in from the probes.

Stan took a peek at both sets of displays in turn. There was undoubtedly something down there. The two sets of data did seem to corroborate each other and the original scan. The substantial feature looked straighter and more regular than undersea cliffs. Thankfully Diana had thought to include a geologist in the expedition. He was currently taking measurements from the screen and looking up his database of underwater rock features. He looked genuinely puzzled.

"How is it looking, Bill?"

"Unusual Dr Havel."

"Call me Stan."

"Sure, thanks."

Stan looked at the scan results unfolding on screen and pointed to an enormous pyramidal structure amongst the regular lines of rock or building.

"What's that, Bill?"

"In truth, I dunno, err, Stan. It could be an underwater volcanic flume. But none have been reported anywhere near here ever before. It's not a volcanic hot spot. It's also a bit regular. Let's stop and measure it. Perhaps the UAVs could get near enough to take a closer look."

The geologist paused the scan and got out a screen measure. Meanwhile, Stan wrote down the GPS coordinates and asked the UAV team to investigate it if possible. One of the techies nodded and gave a thumbs-up as he typed them in.

"Wow. Around 220 to 240 metres. On each of the four sides. Pinpoint height is getting on for 150 metres: my, my. If my memory serves, that's of the order of the Great Pyramid in Giza. I visited there before surveying the Sphinx. Just as well, as I wasn't welcome afterwards. I refused to contradict the geological age proposed by Dr Robert Schoch. Bawass blacklisted me. But I go with my findings, not with a flawed consensus. I better be darn sure about this thing. Any sign of the UAVs?"

Just then, one of the techies standing by the split-screen started gesturing wildly at Stan and Bill. He was called Gary and so far, had only mumbled and giggled in Stan's presence.

"Doc. Come and see this. It's amazing. Pure Cydonia stuff. Not the Sphinx or a face, but clearly a pyramid. It does have some damage, you can see some fallen blocks, but the rest of the surface is smooth, like casing stone. I can't make out the texture or colour at that depth, but it is a regular structure. Got to be man-made. Wow."

Stan momentarily froze at the implications. Then took a rational decision to make the most of this unique opportunity.

"Captain, probe crews. Can we pause at this location and optimise our results. If this is what we think it is, then we need to get the best corroborating evidence that we possibly can. Please."

The ship's Captain and the technicians all nodded. The Captain eased the throttle back to a full stop. The drone crew fiddled with their controls. The sonar probe team also changed their settings.

"All done, Doc. We are fully mapping the anomaly. Full HD. We should be able to match the angle of the sides if it is a pyramid. There should then be no doubt."

Stan nodded. He was still deep in thought. He toyed with contacting Diana but thought that keeping radio silence might be a better course of action at this point. But Diana had sensed otherwise and had come through on the secure line from the HQ ship. The Captain whistled at Stan and gestured him over to the handset.

"Call. Dr Garry. For you, Stan."

"Hiya. What's up, Diana?"

"Hi. Just a feeling you are over something important. I have butterflies in my tummy, and it's not the baby. I feel I should be with you. Is it significant?"

"Yes. Mind-blowing."

"I am coming. How deep?"

"Pretty deep structures. I can't say more. It might be what you, er, saw. But how can you come here?"

"We have the ship. She is geared for diving, and the equipment is sound – or so I am told. The Captain is up for it. The doctor has given me the all-clear to travel. It's my baby as much as our baby is. This ship has past glory for Jacques. Let's give it one more in his memory!"

"You are mad. Can I possibly persuade you not to come?"

"No. We are already on our way. What's your position?"

"I will put the Captain on."

The Captain relayed the coordinates to Diana and then directly onto the commander of the *Nostradamus*. The ex-diving HQ ship corrected its course and set out for open sea.

In a Cuban listening station, a radio operator triangulated the signals and called to his supervisor.

"Comrade. We have a confirmed signal in the forbidden zone. We are attempting to decrypt the messages. We believe the originator is near the Bahamas. We are aware of 2 survey vessels in the region at this moment. One set sail from Miami yesterday at first light. The other one has been moored off of South Bahama. If it is those vessels, we must board and seize the survey evidence."

"Da, da. I will inform the Supreme Leader. And Moscow. We may need back up if it becomes an international incident. "

Both men nodded.

XXIII - Rendezvous

At dawn, the ships met up in open water. The UAV had been brought back aboard, as had the sonar equipment. The engineers had uploaded their results to their cloud storage via the satellite link their benefactor had given them. Point to point there was no leakage. They also copied the sonar scans too.

Diana wasted no time in boarding a speedboat and heading over to the other ship. Despite all she had been through, she virtually jumped up onto the vessel and ran up the stairs to the bridge.

"Hi, everyone. I am not missing this for the world. Can you show me the footage of the main structure please?"

"Here you go, my sweet." Stan beckoned his wife over to the monitor where the HD video of the pyramid-like structure was recorded by the drone's camera.

Diana looked intently before closing her eyes. Some of the memories of her dream, of her life as Messima, came back to her. She remembered the Great Invocation to Amun-Ra. If this was the same structure, then that embossed writing might still be there.

"Do we have clear footage of the structure a few metres from the top?" She asked.

"No, I am afraid we don't. But we do have LIDAR. The analysis came back from our base. It's pretty comprehensive—definitely a pyramid. The top part appears to have an inscription. It appears to be in a script that I can only describe as being quite Sumerian in style and form. I was hoping for hieroglyphs. It looks like I lose my bet." One of the technicians interrupted. The other two looked at each other and did a High five. "Sweet".

Diana went over to the technician's monitor. It surely was The Great Invocation. "Let the light from Amun-Ra come forth into the hearts of all; let love reach down to Earth." She muttered. The shape of the words for Amun-Ra was very distinctive. She could see them. "Bingo! This is the Pyramid of the Light in the centre of Atlán, the circular city in Atlantis." She was ecstatic. All her life she had known that Atlantis had been real. And here she was above it. The hairs on the back of her neck were standing on end.

"Merde! We have company!" The Captain exclaimed.

The whole of the crew and passengers aboard the ship looked out of the windows of the bridge. A submarine had surfaced nearby. Judging by its Cyrillic lettering, it was Russian.

The Captain took an ancient-looking key out of his pocket and opened an old teak drawer below his desk with it. Inside he retrieved three revolvers. He put one in his jacket pocket and handed another to his First Mate. The final one he gave to one of the American technicians. "If they board us, we must fight. We are in international waters, and they have no right to interfere."

Just as things were looking bleak for the survey crew, a Sparrow autogyro appeared. It hovered in front of the window, revealing the intriguing writing along its side of 'Transatlantic Crown Club'.

"Oh great, so now we have James Bond arriving. We don't need a spy on board, not unless he's got an anti-submarine mortar with him. Otherwise, he might as well have brought me curlers!" The Captain spoke and took off his hat to reveal his bald head. The crewman sniggered.

However, the technicians were giving each other more High fives and chatting among themselves.

"What's the gossip gentlemen?" Asked Stan.

"It's Velvet Honeycomb. You know. Your benefactor. They must have seen the data feed."

The tallest of the men ran down the staircase and waved at the autogyro. He gestured for the pilot to go to the back of the ship and land on the helipad there. The strange craft set down on the deck. As soon as the blades had stopped rotating, a woman got out and headed towards the bridge.

A somewhat glamorous dark-haired English woman shook her long dark hair out of her flying helmet. As she arrived, she spoke. "Who is Diana Garry?"

Diana put her hand up and said "I am. And who might you be?"

"I am your mysterious benefactor. But you can call me Tallulah. I must congratulate you on your success. It seems like you have stumbled upon the fabled lost civilisation of Atlantis. Unfortunately, it seems that our Russian friends here were already aware of it. They have orders right from the top to insist that you move off station and return to Port. They are prepared to sink us."

"You have got to be kidding. We are in international waters. How dare they interfere!" Replied Diana.

"It's OK, Doctor Garry. We have formulated a plan that, I hope, will be acceptable to all parties." Tallulah responded.

"Go on, please," Diana spoke again.

"We need to leave as soon as possible. We get to keep the results we have, and they will be invaluable in years to come. My team can study them. We can't tell the world about your discovery quite yet. I hope you understand."

Tallulah made it clear from her speech that there was no room for further negotiation in what she was saying.

Diana was fuming at this. "You have got to be kidding. You can't just drop in here and tell us to forget all about it. That's not fair."

"Life is not fair. Besides, you know the drill. Pont de l'Alma Diana. Don't play innocent with me. If you made all your finds public, the fabric of society would break down. "

Diana flushed. So much for French secrecy. "And if we agree?"

"Nobody dies Diana. And you get to announce that the Phoenicians reached America in the Bronze Age. Predating Columbus, Cabot and even the Vikings. Quite an achievement. I was hoping for some Atlantean technology from your discoveries, but I guess I will have to bribe the guys down in Antarctica instead. It seems the ice hasn't been present there as long as the history books say. So, shall we up anchor and sail back to Miami?"

Diana nodded. Her anger was barely contained as she flexed her hands and dug her nails into her palms until they bled. Stan stared at her, and she at him.

The Captain took back his pistols and locked them up once more. He radioed to the other ship their intention to return to port, then turned the boat sharply around before setting a course back to Miami.

Tallulah had prepared a press release for Diana to use upon her return. She spoke to her in private and smoothed out the objections that Diana had about the whole situation. A lifetime's dream confirmed but forced back into its box. She had wanted to open the lid on Atlantis, but this time Pandora had been foiled.

She wiped away her tears. She had a consolation prize. But in taking it, a small part of her died inside. She had heard tales of cover-ups. Out of place objects and advanced technologies found by other Archaeologists. But she had dismissed them. Yet here she was accepting a large bursary on behalf of her University from a woman who had just done a deal with the Kremlin. She felt sick.

XXIV – Shelved

D iana had not had any part of her previous digs 'black shelved' before. But she knew that it could happen to anyone in her profession. She suspected that the Gunung Padang site in Indonesia had been shut down after the team there announced to the world that they believed that their site included a pyramid 10-20,000 years old. It didn't fit in with the 'Golden Crescent' model and nor did an Atlantean site being confirmed in the sea between Cuba and the Bahamas.

So, was she to be a good girl and stick with Tallulah's plan and avoid professional suicide – or worse – or tell the truth and become a maverick like her father and the others whose careers had been ruined.

As she sat at her desk on her last full day onboard the ship that had been her home for the previous few months before and after her near-fatal accident she told herself that if it was just her decision and her future at stake she would have exposed the site of the Atlantean pyramid temple to the world. But with Stan's future and that of their child at risk, then she would have to play it safe. At least for now. She had 'accidentally' kept a back up of the scan results and as much of the HD footage as would fit on her USB stick—one for her memoirs or a later point when the pretence was finally up. The truth cannot be hidden forever.

She thought back to her long and very lucid dream while in her coma. The details were so precise and yet so damaging as a concept to many of her colleagues and Egyptologists who relied upon the sanctity of the current model of civilisation.

Even the discovery of Gobleki Tepe some years ago with its high-status carvings and carbon dating to some 12,000 years ago did not seem to worry those who kept control of the historical agenda. Its proximity to the biblical Garden of Eden and the Fertile Crescent in the Middle East did not make it a threat. Earlier finds in the Americas or Asia did rather upset it.

The pyramid she had seen in her dream, the pyramid that seemed to match it and its inscription on the seabed off of Cuba could all undermine the delicate balance that history currently held.

Pyramids were a fascinating subject to her. When she was a schoolgirl, she had a poster of the Great Pyramid of Giza. It sat uncomfortably next to Take That on her wall. She had wrongly believed that there were only pyramids in Egypt. But then she heard about the stepped pyramids in Mexico and South America.

The Temple of the Feathered Serpent at Teotihuacan in Mexico was truly spectacular. She had never visited Egypt or Mexico, but she had been to places that reminded her of those sites. She had happened across the hill in Bosnia where a few years later, a maverick archaeologist named Osmanagich announced to the world that he had discovered a giant pyramid under the hillside. She got tingles down her spine on hearing that news since she had pointed out to her father that the hill in question looked just like a pyramid as they drove past it on a tourist trip and even he had laughed it off.

During her time convalescing after her accident, Diana spent a lot of time looking for clues relating to pyramids and other things she had glimpsed in Atlantis.

She discovered that the problem with pyramids wasn't that they didn't exist across the world, as they indeed now appear to have been a common feature, but in the names that they had been given.

Even the word 'pyramid' was derived from a Greek word, 'pyramis' describing the shape of the Egyptian pyramids. The Egyptian name was actually 'Mer'. The capstone of a pyramid was called 'ben-ben', as was the tip of the obelisks such as 'Cleopatra's Needle' now found in London.

The term 'ben-ben' related to the sacred benben stone found in the temple of the Sun at Heliopolis. We don't even know where the name 'Mer' originated. In Proto-Indo-European languages, 'Mer' means 'to rub away harm' or possibly ward away harm. Taking the concept one further, if the pyramids were initially decorated with symbols and knowledge, then one symbol could easily have been the 'Eye of Ra' which included an eye. In many cultures surrounding Egypt and the Mediterranean, the eye is used as a talisman to ward off evil or keep away harm.

In her trip to Thailand and other parts of Asia as a backpacker in her year out as a youth, she had spotted features on ancient temples that matched pyramids elsewhere. The serpents or 'Nagas' on Buddhist temples were very similar to the snakes on the pyramids in Mexico. Yet perceived wisdom was that there had been no contact between these races in ancient times.

At one ruined temple in Chiang Mai in Thailand, she had seen a large tower, called a 'chedi' or 'stupa', where the relics of Buddha were kept that resembled a stepped pyramid. This temple was called Wat Chedi Leung. It meant 'temple of the enormous stupa'.

Other Buddhist and Hindu temples in Thailand, Cambodia and India that she saw held a resemblance to pyramids. Even the pagoda structures in China were often tall towers that started wider at their base and gradually narrowed further up, ending up with a triangular section roof on the top.

In Biblical texts, the 'Tower of Babel' is thought to have been a ziggurat as found in various sites around Babylon and Syria. Ziggurats are often wholly ruined. But those that remain look like a cross between a large tower and a stepped pyramid.

Even near to her own childhood home in the south-west of England that is more famous for its ancient stone circles of Stonehenge and Avebury, there is a conical man-made hill that is comparable to the pyramids - Silbury Hill.

Recent digs on other mounds used to believed to have been built by the Normans as part of their castles have been identified as potential ancient druidic mounds dating back much earlier than the 11th century AD.

She had once made the mistake of asking questions about the different forms of pyramids across the world to her lecturer at University. He had shot her down in flames. He had said. "Diana, my girl, if you want to get on as an Archaeologist, don't go out on a limb by asking questions that are at odds with the current consensus view. It never ends well for those that do."

She had remained wary and had avoided getting into situations where she might end up challenging her colleagues.

For some reason, she had become drawn to the Bahamas and its intriguing marble pillars. In her conscious mind, she had never imagined for a minute that she might get pulled into proving the myth of Atlantis. But perhaps her unconscious mind had hoped it would locate Atlantis with her help. It was intriguing, but now she was in an ethical dilemma.

To satisfy Tallulah and the Archaeological director at the Atlantic University of Miami, Professor Chuck Morris, Diana was tasked with separating the definite Phonecian era finds from any earlier evidence of Atlantean activity at the Bahamas dig site. The other expedition towards Cuba never happened. The divers were bought off yet again.

Just as she was finishing compiling a list of artefacts to be published in the Archaeological paper and listing the others in an inventory to be black-shelved for the director, Jerry knocked on the door.

"Miss Diana, I have made you an espresso, just how you like it. It's using Cuban coffee beans – I have a source." Jerry held her finger up to her lips as she whispered the last part.

Diana chuckled as she held out her hand for the small cup of coffee. "My lips are sealed. I am good with secrets." She decided it was better to laugh about it than to cry.

"I'm gonna miss you when you've gone back to England. Promise you'll keep in touch and send me pictures of your gorgeous little person when he or she is born."

"Yes, of course, I will. I have grown very fond of you and the rest of the team. I am sure you will all go on to achieve great things at other sites once you all graduate."

"Thank you. Finding these Phoenician things here has been my career highlight so far. Just think, Columbus might have had a map that had been drawn by those guys when he sailed to the good ole US of A. It's truly amazing."

"It certainly is. And who knows how much earlier too."

"It's a shame we never found anything that turned out to be Atlantean. That would have turned an epic dig into a turning point in world history!"

Diana's stomach went tight again as Jerry uttered those words. "Yes indeed, Jerry. Yes, indeed."

Jerry waved and let herself back out again.

Diana finished both lists a few minutes afterwards and emailed them to Tallulah and the Director.

The black-shelved artefacts, Diana was assured, were to be sent to a special section of the Smithsonian for further study out of the public eye. She very much hoped they wouldn't be destroyed like she feared some other 'Out of Place Artefacts' had been.

She was risking a lot by keeping copies of some of the photos taken by the team of the banned items. She had zipped and encrypted them as a binary file under a randomised name. Fingers crossed they would stay undiscovered.

A small kick in her tummy from her baby reminded her of the importance of keeping to the deal.

She had at least avoided taking what she considered 'blood money' for her silence or accepting a promotion to another University sponsored by Tallulah.

As she daydreamed back to her undergraduate days, she recalled accidentally attending a Fortean Society meeting by a keen amateur historian. She couldn't remember his name, but he had set up an old Agfa slide projector and carousel with a set of 35mm slides to talk through.

He was talking about out of place artefacts in archaeology and items that hinted of Atlantis.

In one slide, he had a picture of a bird that looked like a modern-day glider that had been found in an ancient Egyptian tomb. He remarked that it could have been a 'Vimana' that was mentioned in the ancient Hindu text known as the Mahabharata. He added that a replica was made from the original and it flew perfectly, thus proving that Egyptians knew aerodynamics and presumably flight. He also had a slide of temple hieroglyphs that appeared to show submarines and other technology.

When she was finished with her daydream, she started packing up her things ready for leaving the ship the following day. As she did so, her phone rang. It was from the director's office. She held her breath as she answered. "Yes".

"Diana, good to speak to you again. Fine work on the paper and artefacts. We want to hold a press conference next week to announce your Phoenician discoveries at the dig site. We will hold it in the University Grand Hall. Stan and the rest of your team can be there too. We'll have a party afterwards to thank you all for your efforts. I hope we can rely upon your, um, discretion?"

"Of course." Diana sighed.

"Fantastic. Thursday next week, around lunchtime. We'll confirm it all when you are all back stateside. The crates are all secured and screened by the Bahamian authorities?"

"Yes, they are Director. Two sets, as agreed."

"Thank you again, Diana. I'll be speaking to you soon then. Goodbye."

"Bye." She put her phone down and turned it off. She was about to cry when Stan put his head through the door.

"How are you doing my darling? And how's little Janey?".

"Oh, she's fine. I suspect she is a girl as I've not been very sick with her and I think with boys it's often a problem to be carrying two sets of hormones." She replied.

"We're going to break out some drinks for an end of dig party aboard. You look like you could do with one, but of course, we've got a whole host of mocktails for you and the other non-drinkers aboard. I would show solidarity with you by not drinking, but somebody has sent over a crate of Budweiser Budvar from Czechia. It would be rude not to drink it."

"Yes, rude not to. I'll let you this one time you git. This is all your fault, you know." She pointed to her tummy.

"Oh, yes. It takes two to tango my darling. I didn't hear you complaining."

Diana flushed.

"I just want to be getting home now. All the fun's gone out of this situation."

"Yes, I know what you mean. But we'll bounce back. We've still pushed back boundaries here. Just not all the ones we hoped for."

"Agreed."

XXV – Press

The morning of the press conference, Diana got up from bed in her Miami hotel room, leaving Stan sleeping.

She had a shower and carefully washed around the site of her wound where the stitches had now been removed. Dabbing the towel gently so as not to knock her scar, Diana dried herself off then went to her wardrobe to select an outfit. She giggled as she chose her horizontal striped black and white dress. It did look like a prison uniform in some respects. A non-verbal protest at the constraints she was now under in keeping the secrets of Atlantis under wraps for at least a little longer.

Stan smiled at her as she returned to the dressing table to do her makeup. He headed to the bathroom, humming as he went. Diana was not in nearly such a good mood. She was less than happy with what she had to say at the press conference. But lives were potentially at stake. She would play her part but would give clues to her real views. She would wear the Templar brooch with the equilateral cross motif and her dolphin earrings. Both symbols linked in her mind to Atlantis. Her Egyptian ankh would complete the set, however, mismatched it might appear.

Stan had put on his blazer with the white trim. He looked like Number Five from the classic TV series 'The Prisoner'. He had the same idea, though they hadn't discussed it. Perhaps their costumes and body language would spark conspiracy theories in years to come, much like Neil Armstrong's curious use of words during the Moon landings. 'That's one small step for man, one giant leap for mankind.' Was it nerves that made him omit the 'a' from 'for a man's or was it a clue that it wasn't such a giant leap after all? Would we ever know now he had passed away? Diana finished her makeup with her slightly curious purple toned lipstick and matching eye shadow.

After a brief breakfast where Stan packed in a full stack of American pancakes with maple syrup and Diana managed a croissant with a robust Americano, it was time to head around the corner for the news conference in the Grand Hall of Miami's Atlantic University.

The hall was a mixture of contemporary technology and faded Art Deco architecture. The stage was being prepared for the press conference with banners made up for the occasion. There were images of the Phoenician artefacts that had been discovered during the dig—none of the older stuff.

The seats were starting to fill up in the auditorium. Interestingly near to Tallulah was a man who had more than a passing resemblance to Edward Dusk. So perhaps he was the mysterious benefactor after all.

She would be watching him closely.

Some thickset slavic men were also sitting prominently. They looked quite familiar. They appeared to be the same two men who had admired the spire of Salisbury cathedral during the spy poisoning scandal in England a few years previously. That must have been a deliberate attempt to say that the FSB is watching you. No heroics. Diana swallowed.

Stan tapped her on the shoulder and whispered in her ear. She looked around and could see Professor Heinz Schmidt in the audience. He hadn't told them he would be in town. It was nice to see a friendly face in the crowd. The rest was made up of the press, archaeologists and a few conspiracy people. Al James was there too. "Oh, great." Diana heard herself saying as she saw him.

With the audience in place, the conference was preparing to

start. From its makeup, Diana knew what line of questioning was likely. She would evade any awkward lines of discussion and stick to the key points that were consistent with the Phoenician findings. She didn't relish the prospect of a horrible radioactive death if the cathedral groupies didn't like her answers.

The University Chancellor had arrived on the stage and walked straight up to the podium to give his speech.

"Ladies and Gentlemen, colleagues, academics and members of the world's press. Very few times in my career have I been present at pivotal moments in history. But today is one such time. Columbus Day may never be quite the same again. Today we change the history of the Americas and plant a middle eastern flag on our continent. The irony of this is not entirely lost on me. My esteemed colleague, the Director of Archaeology Professor Chuck Morris, will give you the full details. I am sure you will agree it is all quite remarkable. "

The Chancellor left the podium and sat back next to his wife. Her red dress and grey hair contrasted greatly with his formal black suit and wispy black hair.

Chuck Morris wandered up to the lectern. His hair was unusually tidy, and his shirt and tie made him look much more serious than his regular comfortable corduroy trousers and polo shirts. He turned back and smiled at Diana before addressing the audience.

"Ladies and Gentlemen. Others. Welcome. Rarely in my long career have I been given the opportunity to make an announcement that pushed our understanding of history to another level. But today is one such occasion. We have conclusive proof and confirmed dating evidence that a Phoenician port was established in South Bimini in the Bahamas."

The audience gasped. The editor of 'The Modern Archaeologist' magazine, Clarence de Pinks, shook his head in disbelief.

"Not only that, but the earliest piece of evidence that we have found is 4,500 years old, so corresponds to the very start of those sea-faring people from around modern-day Lebanon. We can only speculate as to why they were here, of course. But as we know, there were many resources in North America and Central America in antiquity as well as in the Bahamas themselves that might have been traded for goods from the Middle East. It might even go on to explain why some mummies in Egypt have been found to contain traces of tobacco that were not native to their region but are native to ours. Though that might be too controversial to speculate on at this point."

De Pinks nodded his head vigorously as he was frantically jotting down notes. Al James was smiling. The Professor continued speaking.

"But enough speculation. The fact is that the Phoenicians were here in the Americas long before Columbus, Cabot or even the Vikings. We have artefacts, we have marble columns, and we have statues attributable to the ancient seafarers from around Tyre."

Chuck gestured to Diana to come up and join him.

"Here is the dig Director who discovered these items in the sand and shallow waters of the Bahamas. All the way from England and seconded to us from Bath Sulis University. Please give a big hand to Doctor Diana Garry."

The audience clapped and cheered. Mostly. Both Clarence de Pinks and Al James seemed somewhat subdued compared with the others.

Diana took to the podium as Chuck patted her on the back and headed back to his seat.

The lights dimmed, and a large screen descended behind her. An elegant pillar of marble filled the screen.

"Hello. I can see that many of you may be sceptical about our finds and our conclusions. But let me be clear. The dating evidence ranges from 4,500 years ago to 3,000 years ago—the classic Phoenician period. The pillar behind me appears Greek in style, yet it predates the Greeks by at least 500 years. Thermoluminescence dating of a sample dated this to between 1000 and 1100 BCE."

The picture changed to that of the small orichalcum statue behind her.

"And this statue, in reality just a few centimetres tall, was covered in a biological deposit that has been carbon-dated by three independent laboratories to 4500 BCE. And we have other items of pottery – generally shards of amphora (bottles) – that demonstrate continuous habitation of the site between the two dates. Two broken stone anchors of likely Middle Eastern origin were found out to sea from our dig site and not far from the so-called Bimini Road. Lending credibility to the prior conjecture that the Bimini Road may have been a quay complex at a time when sea levels were lower than today."

Diana paused from speaking as a picture of one of the stone anchors faded from view as the lights were turned up and the screen disappeared from behind her.

"I can say it has been an honour to work on this dig alongside my colleagues from the Atlantic University and my husband, Doctor Stanislav Harvel."

A few claps and cheers broke out from amongst the audience.

"I am sure you all have many questions." Diana paused then gulped as a sea of hands raised. Thankfully each delegate was holding a cardboard number issued to them at the desk on entry.

"Number 25."

Clarence de Pinks stood up to ask his question. "Doctor Garry. Congratulations on this impressive gallery of artefacts. Can you be sure this wasn't carried here in more modern times for onward sale to the faker Father Crespi?"

Diana smiled and looked the man straight in the eyes.

"We can be quite sure that these artefacts have lain undisturbed for many hundreds of years under deposit layers consistent with their surroundings and confirmed by large scale LIDAR traces of the dig site and beyond. Only the faint edges of the items were initially visible in many cases, and they had to be excavated carefully by diggers or divers from the sediment. We are releasing a peer-reviewed scientific paper of our findings to be published in the next issue of the 'Journal of Scientific Archaeology and Antiquities'. We will provide copies for you as you leave."

Mr de Pinks seemed dumbstruck and just nodded.

"Number 66." Diana picked Al James' hand.

"Hi. Al James. I applaud your discoveries here and your little cover story. But I have it on excellent authority that you discovered remnants of Atlantis off of the coast of Cuba while you were aboard a charter vessel. So please, spare me any more of this charade and confess the truth. Your team have proof of the 'mythical' Island if Atlantis but you don't have the guts to tell us. Deny it why don't you!"

Diana had flushed red at this. One of the crew must have sold their story.

"That's an interesting interpretation of recent events. However, we were using geological mapping tools to trace the edge of the tectonic plates between the Bahamas and Cuba to establish the rate of tectonic plate subduction between our survey and a prior survey done some twenty years ago. Factoring in the so-called ice age rebound the results are consistent with our site being a waterside settlement for the period up to just before 1000 BCE. We can probably rustle up those results for you."

Al James appeared even angrier than usual. He shouted "Cover-up. Atlantis was real. These liars know it. They have been paid off. It's all a charade!" With that, he turned away and stormed out of the press conference. He had made his point.

Diana continued almost unphased. Her stomach was sick at being called out by James, but the cover story sounded plausible and had been war-gamed by her and Professor Morris the previous day while Tallulah looked on impassively at the pair of them.

The press conference concluded a few minutes later, and the delegates were free to mingle together over a light buffet with some champagne. Diana noticeably relaxed as Stan came over to greet her along with Heinz.

"Congratulations, my dear. I am very proud of you. You have another major achievement against your name without the blight of controversy. Ignore men like Al James. He was out if order with his accusations, I am sure. Even if you had in reality discovered Atlantis, you would not be announcing it today. As I did not back in the 1980s with my team. Some things are better to remain unsaid."

Diana's jaw dropped at Heinz's revelation. She had no idea.

XXVI - Life

Back in England in her parents' study overlooking Corfe Castle, the cuckoo clock ticking and the late summer sun falling on her notebook she cast her mind back to the press conference in Miami where she announced the Phoenician link to the world. She was dazed by it all, yet had to bite her tongue not to reveal the real facts. The attendance by the Russians who looked like assassins reminded her that Atlantis was still off-limits. For now. The offer of a chair at The Atlantic University of Miami was tempting, but America was no place to bring up kids. So, she declined and returned to the UK to continue to study the artefacts from her Bahamian dig.

As she put her pen down, she got a jarring sensation in her abdomen. There was a sensation of water dripping down her leg. Another round of contractions had started. And now her waters had broken.

"Stan, Mother! I think it's time for me to be going. My waters have broken, and my contractions are less than five minutes. Are my things in the boot?"

"Coming dear. Let's help you down to the car. You can sit on this towel. Stan – here are my keys, you can have the honour of driving your wife to the hospital. I will sit in the back quietly." Replied her mother.

Both Stan and Diana laughed at her mother's comments. She was never quiet. And with her first grandchild imminent it seemed even less likely.

The drive to Poole hospital maternity unit had been well-practised, but with the holiday traffic, it still took nearly thirty minutes. By the time they arrived, Diana was panting and in discomfort as her contractions neared four minutes apart.

The midwife on duty on the maternity department desk had a quick look at Diana and summoned a porter to take her straight upstairs to the labour suite.

On the maternity ward, another midwife took Diana into one of the rooms to examine her. She had to strip below the waist for the exam. "Oh, yes, nicely dilated. Not long now, dear. You better clamber up on this bed and make yourself comfortable. Not that it really will be." She said. Looking at Stan she added "Nice to have the support of your man, but he'll be comfortable enough. He gets the easy part."

The midwife was, of course, quite right. Diana went into full-blown labour a few minutes later. Feeling like her body was being torn apart as she attempted to squeeze something the size of a melon out of an aperture the size of a grape, the gruelling ordeal seemed to go on forever. She refused pain killers so as not to risk her baby, so she felt it all. Her lower abdomen ached and burned like never before. The waves of contractions intensified, and she pushed when the midwife or Stan shouted "Push!", but the youngster was showing all the stubbornness of its mother, grandmother and father all put together. Diana's mother was calmly knitting some little green booties while sat on a seat at the bottom of the bed. She was occasionally looking up. "You took 12 hours, Tara 11 and Aphrodite 10. I can't see you'll be less than 8." She helpfully remarked some 5 hours into Diana's labour.

"Oh God, shoot me, Ow, ow, ow, ow!" Diana called out soon after.

"Stick with it, my darling," Stan replied.

"That's effing easy for you to say. Do you think I'm even able to stop now? Owwww!" She snapped.

The cycle repeated several times before Diana repositioned herself, legs splayed even further, she screamed: "Out you come!". Panting and pushing with mighty breaths and mighty pushes, she timed her exertions perfectly with the latest round of contractions to manage to push the baby's head out of her. With some coaxing by the midwife and more pushes its shoulders, body and feet came out too.

Stan stared in awe at what looked like a purple-red fish deposited at the bottom of the bed. The midwife wiped its mouth, and the baby let out an enormous cry to start up its lungs. The midwife clamped the umbilical cord once it had stopped pulsing, injected Diana with syntometrine to help her uterus contract and coaxed her to give birth to her placenta. With the placenta on the nearby trolley, she snipped the cord and handed the baby to its mother, Diana.

"It's a girl! She's beautiful!" Said Stan.

"I thought it would be. You were less sick than with a boy. The same as me." Said her mother.

Diana just wanted to sleep. She was a bloody mess. Her bottom hurt, all her muscles ached, and her back was in agony. But the baby had other ideas. She clamped on to her mother's breast as soon as she realised what it was.

"Garr! Ow, ow!" Diana cried.

The midwife came over and showed Diana how to cradle the baby while breastfeeding. Stan looked on in wonder at his newest family member. Diana's mother came over and peered closely at her granddaughter. "Oh, can I capture this moment on my phone?" she asked.

"Yes, I'll just cover myself up a bit, and hide her dignity too. OK, go ahead, Mummy. Is Stan in too?"

"Oh yes, lean in Stanislav," she said, slightly grudgingly.

And so it was that Ruby Louise Francis Havel was born just before 1 am on 16th August weighing 7 ½ pounds.

Diana had to get to grips with motherhood. She hadn't realised just how messy it would be for her as well as for her daughter. She had to have several stitches, which tended to catch and burn as she tried to sleep. And just when she became comfortable, her darling daughter would demand a feed, or a change, or both. It was exhausting.

Stan did his best. He attended to her needs during visiting hours and brought in balloons and teddies that he'd bought or that were sent by well-wishers. The cuddly mermaid sent over by Tallulah was not too well received and was at the bottom of the teddy pile.

After another three whole days, mother and baby were deemed well enough to go home. Diana had to undergo some extra tests to ensure she was OK on top of her accident. She required some extra vitamins but was otherwise surprisingly healthy.

Stan had hired a car and brought the vehicle carry-cot along so that he could bring his wife and daughter home in style. And by home, this would be their small rented terraced house in one of the suburbs of Bath. It was an hour and a half journey but did mean that they could all be together now that he too was working at Bath Sulis University like his wife.

He proudly carried his daughter inside, with his wife holding his arm to steady herself after the journey—home at last.

• •

XXVII – Celebrations

I t was not to be an extended stay at home as the first Saturday in September was to be the wedding of Tara and Amelia.

Friday morning, after Ruby's first feed, the new family headed back down towards Corfe Castle from their Bath home. Being early, they were able to avoid much of the morning rush-hour as they drove down to the coast in the car Stan had again hired for the weekend. Diana initially sat in the front while Ruby was sleeping. But their respite was short-lived as the insatiable needs of their new daughter forced them to pull over in a layby so that Diana could go into the back of the car and attend to her baby. It was exhausting, and Diana was not looking or feeling her best by the time they pulled up outside Diana's childhood home in view of the beautiful ruined Corfe Castle back in Dorset in the south-west of England.

Enid Blyton had loved the village and the wider area a generation before Diana's father came along as a young archaeologist and fell in love with the place. Diana and her two sisters Aphrodite and Tara had grown up here and had played in and around the slopes of the castle all of their childhood. The same place she had broken her arm in her father's dig's pit. Even now her parents lived here as her father had retired from active lecturing and was now resident archaeologist at the castle. His career as a maverick had never gained him the recognition that he deserved. However, he was admirably proud of his daughter Diana's accolades at both Chenonceau in France and the site in the Bahamas. "Best he not know about the Cuban incident," she thought to herself as she unbuckled her seatbelt and leant over to undo Ruby's travel seat from the rear of the car. Ruby was, of course, looking downright angelic as she prepared to nap now that her mother had changed, fed, burped and comforted her all through the journey. "I love you, my sweet. But you drive me mad!" she whispered as Ruby gurgled while opening and closing her eyes.

Grandpa Garry had put his trowel down for the day as he was already at the door with a soft rabbit toy from the nearby National Trust shop for his granddaughter. He was very proud to welcome this new addition to the family, on the eve of welcoming yet another female to the family once Amelia married Tara in the grounds of the castle.

Diana and her family were staying at the Marden's house next door. The Marden family had been neighbours throughout Diana's lifetime. Their son Martin had once had a crush on Diana when they were both ten years old. They used to climb trees together in the woods at the bottom of the hill or splash in the brook. Both of them would come home bruised and covered in mud, much to their mothers' annoyance. But the potential romance between the two had ended when Martin had tried to kiss his tomboy friend, and she had responded by punching his nose to give him a nose bleed. They had kept a wary distance after that. Thankfully their families had remained friends, and now with Martin long moved out Diana, her husband and baby daughter would be staying in his old bedroom. They carried the travel cot upstairs along with the bare minimum two huge bags of baby supplies as Grandpa watched Ruby in the Garry family's front room. Chow-Chow, Grandma's dog had been relegated to her kennel.

Aphrodite had already arrived and unusually was not lamenting her latest break up to Tara and Amelia on the settee. By the time that Diana appeared, Aphrodite was modelling her purple bride's maid dress. As Diana was otherwise occupied with Ruby, it had been decided that Aphrodite would be Maid of Honour despite Diana already being Amelia's sister-in-law as Amelia was Stan's sister. The hen party had been suitably raucous as a weekend for both Tara's friends and Amelia's friends from Czechia. It had started in a gay bar in Playa del Ingles in Gran Canaria in the Spanish Canary Islands. An Irish girl had taken a liking to Aphrodite, and the pair had disappeared late into the evening leaving Tara, Amelia and the others to go on to a pole dancing club where the girls had out whistled the boys, before ending up doing Karaoke into the early hours at another bar.

Diana had heard three different stories, having spoken to both of her sisters and heard Amelia's account via Stan. She didn't know what to believe or if Aphrodite was about to come out to them. All she knew was that there was a late addition to the guest list, Aphrodite's friend Sian.

Diana's bridesmaid dress was hanging up behind the door to the lounge, so she took it and went to her old room to try it on. Thankfully it had been made flexible in the tummy area and a little forgiving in its shape, so she was able to put it on without a great struggle, and secure it to hide her remaining loose tummy skin and to obscure her nursing bra. It could also be partially unclipped to allow her to breastfeed Ruby if required (as seemed likely). She returned down to the others and gave them a quick twirl.

Diana's mother, Karen, came in and hugged her youngest daughter.

"Glad to see you looking beautiful in that bridesmaid's dress Diana. You've been through so many ups and downs this year. Welcome back home, my dear. Would you like a cuppa?"

"I'd love an Americano," Diana replied.

"Not while you're breastfeeding my granddaughter, you won't. All caffeine's a bad idea. How about a camomile tea?"

"I guess you're right. Just try and keep me awake through the service tomorrow if I get as much sleep as I've had the last few weeks - like a couple of hours a night. I'm wearing my full makeup tomorrow. I know I look an awful sight."

"You and the other girls kept me up enough when you were babies. I don't think you look too bad considering. But I'll get you that tea. Anybody else?" Karen ended by asking the others, but they all shook their heads. She went out to the kitchen to make it for Diana.

Diana sat down in the remaining armchair and faced the other women. "So, what's the timetable for tomorrow?"

Aphrodite and Tara took turns in explaining the details to Diana as she nodded or occasionally made a few comments or observations.

Diana and Aphrodite went up to change out of their bridesmaid's dresses. While up there their mother beckoned them over to Tara's room, where she unzipped the wedding dress to show them. Both of the sisters gave a satisfying 'Ooh' as they looked at the delicate lace details on the otherwise very modern dress that Tara had chosen. Amelia hadn't seen it and had her's at the Marden's house. Stan had looked at it and had indicated his approval to Diana over it a few days earlier. His best man's suit was a dinner jacket with a colourful waistcoat and bow tie. His mother's dress was going to be in leaf green as she wanted a contrast to the bridesmaids as she was going to walk her daughter up the aisle in the absence of her late husband, Vaclav. Her brother was not available to come to Amelia's wedding since he had a lucrative fishing trip that weekend and was unable or unwilling to cancel it.

By late evening, after the journey, the endless feeds of Ruby and the time with her family, Diana was ready for bed, so excused herself. She would need to be up early for the wedding preparations and makeup artist who was coming to make up the bride and her sisters first thing in the morning.

When the 7 am alarm went off, Ruby started screaming immediately. Her mum had to get up to rush and pick her up to comfort her. Both of them were soon back in bed with Ruby sucking away at her mother's sore nipple. "Ow, ow, careful Ruby. I'm dreading when you start to get teeth."

At 7:30, Diana was able to go over to her parents' house and take Ruby with her, plus the bare essentials for the day with a baby. She brought with her the baby sling she had bought, carefully colour-matched to her purple bridesmaid's dress.

Amelia went to the Marden's house where her brother Stan was getting ready in his tuxedo, and where their mother had just arrived from her hotel in nearby Swanage.

Both the brides wanted to keep their dress secret from the other, though they had agreed on a pearl-white colour for them both, to look better in photographs. They had also borrowed items from their respective mothers plus found blue garters to wear, as was the English tradition. Amelia and her family would act as the 'groom's party' since she was marrying the local girl, but Tara would retain her 'Garry' surname and Amelia would become Amelia Garry. It seemed fair since Diana was now Mrs Havel (Although professionally she was still Doctor Garry).

Diana's father Peter Garry was dressed in his best grey suit, a red jumper with a white shirt and National Trust tie. He was calmly sat in his usual chair, blissfully unaware of the wedding pandemonium unfolding around him with all the current female members of his family. Diana spotted him sitting quietly so gave him Ruby to cuddle. "This brings back memories." He said to her as she dashed away to re-join her sisters and help zip Tara into her dress.

"Darn thing must have shrunk!" Tara exclaimed as Aphrodite, Diana and their mother Karen all tried to force the zip at the back of the wedding dress to close.

"Have you eaten breakfast yet?" Asked Diana.

"No. Why?" Replied Tara.

"Don't then. And nip to the loo before we try again. I have some baby oil we can use on your back to help it all go in." Diana added.

"Jesus. OK. As long as we get the deposit back on this dress."

Tara disappeared for a few minutes and reappeared again for a second attempt.

"I took my bra off. That should help. I can also lift my arms at the appropriate time." She offered.

Diana massaged her oldest sister's back in baby oil, then wiped off the excess with a baby wipe and stood ready for action once more.

"Let's try again. Three, two, one, go!" Diana exclaimed.

This time the zip shot up and Diana's hand slapped the back of Tara's head.

"Ow. But I guess it is up at least. Can I eat my lunch? Do you think?"

Diana, Aphrodite and their mum looked at each other without answering the question.

Tara said "I see. Thanks."

At that moment Trudie the hair and make-up artist arrived, so the two bridesmaids both raced down to the door.

The hair and makeup artist was exquisitely made up and was wearing an eccentric feather boa on her head. Aphrodite showed her up the stairs and into the main bedroom where Tara was now sat ready for the next stage of her preparation. Trudie got out her various brushes, foundation and eye shadow containers and set them down carefully on the dressing table. She then took a careful look at Tara's recently coiffured hair, nails and face before getting out her brush and hair grips. She brushed Tara's hair carefully to make it all immaculate, pinned it in place then set to work on her makeup. Twenty minutes later she was looking beautiful in her wedding dress.

Aphrodite was next up. Her expensive hair cut proved easy to tweak, and her make up seemed to glide on so that ten minutes later, she also was looking resplendent in her bridesmaid's outfit.

Trudie took a sharp intake of breath when she looked carefully at Diana and said: "Mum next, I think." So, she worked on Karen instead. Their mother was wearing an uncharacteristic blue dress after what happened at Diana's wedding. Fifteen minutes later, she too was looking immaculate.

Finally, she set to work on Diana. "New mum?" she asked.

"Yes," Diana replied.

"Thought so. You probably need some extra iron tablets. But for now, we'll put the colour back in your face with a deeper foundation, some contouring and blush."

Twenty minutes later, Diana was looking like her old self, beautifully presented in her purple bridesmaid's dress.

Karen paid Trudie, and the girl popped round to the next-door house to work her magic on Amelia and her mother.

With an hour to go before they needed to head over to the castle grounds, the weather was looking fine for them. It was a late summer day with the first smell of Autumn in the light breeze.

Karen's friends were already over at the venue, with some of her husband's colleagues just tweaking the arrangements and roping off sections of the grounds for their exclusive use during the service. The guests were being ushered into the castle grounds. By special arrangement, the castle flagpole was flying the rainbow Pride flag, and the guest tents were trimmed in English flags, Czech flags, rainbow, lesbian pink, mauve, purple and white flags plus blue white and pink transgender pride flags. It was very colourful. And so were many of the guests.

The local vicar had long since fallen out with Tara's family over his "Just visiting?" questions every time they went to a service a few times a year. So, he was not going to be officiating. Instead, one of Tara's LGBTQ+ friends from a very progressive church in London was going to conduct the service. Hawk was the first gender-fluid priest to be accepted in the church and they never disappointed, today wearing a cassock, tights, Doc Marten boots, rainbow nails and matching beard with Mohican hair dyed purple. They were now testing the microphone ready for the service to start.

At the appointed hour Stan texted Diana to tell her that his family were heading over to the venue. As it was so close, they were just able to walk, so no cars were required. Diana peered out of the window in time to see their backs and Amelia in her heels towering over her mother and Stan as they made their way up the hill and across to the castle grounds.

Diana had just had time to change Ruby's nappy, give her a last feed, burp her, go to the loo herself and hang the baby sling around her left side ready for their journey to the church.

Thankfully Tara's wedding dress train was not too long, so Aphrodite was able to carry it while Diana reacquainted herself with the low heels of the sandals she was wearing under her bridesmaid's dress. After several months of flats and never with a baby attached, she came near to twisting her foot several times. But with Ruby with her, she was cautious not to fall over.

As Tara's party neared the entrance into the castle grounds, the Swanage LGBTQ+ Pride Band started playing 'Here Comes the Bride'. Stan and his mother had already walked Amelia up to the makeshift altar of rainbow coloured Perspex up the slope towards the castle keep, and now she was standing waiting with Stan to her right. Her mother sat just behind him, along with a mixture of family and friends, sat on both sides.

Tara's father led his daughter up the aisle to the front, with her sisters and mother walking up behind her. The guests gasped at her beautiful pearl white dress with exquisite silk filigree flowers and lace trim. It contrasted nicely with Amelia's similarly coloured pearl dress, but in her case, it was exquisitely embroidered with dragonflies in beige.

As the two women stood together at the altar, the guests sat down, and so did Tara's sisters.

Diana managed to spot that Ruby was about to cry out and so she gave her one of her fingers to suck. The baby seemed quite happy with that and thankfully stayed quiet throughout. Stan had looked back to see his wife and daughter seat themselves at the front of the bridal party.

Hawk began their wedding speech.

"Dearly beloved, we are gathered together in the sight of God and this congregation to join in matrimony these two ladies. Can there be anything more beautiful than the union of two roses in the act of marriage? Truly not. And dare anyone to come forward and give reasons why this union cannot happen?"

There was silence.

"Then. Repeat after me. I, Amelia Tatiana Havel take you, Tara Fitzgerald Garry, to my lawful wedded wife. To have and to hold from this day forward until death do us part."

Amelia repeated the line, stumbling briefly over Tara's middle name. Stan passed her the ring to place on Tara's finger.

"And do you, Tara Fitzgerald Garry take this woman Amelia Tatiana Havel to your lawful wedded wife?"

Tara answered, "I do". Stan passed Tara the ring to place on Amelia's finger.

"Then, by the power vested in me by the Progressive Church of Love, Equality and Respect, I now pronounce you wife and wife. You may now kiss the brides."

The two newlyweds kissed to the cheers of the guests while Hawk clapped them. The women and their mothers were then beckoned to go and sign the register. Hawk smiled when they all returned. The band had been playing a medley of Beatles songs concluding with 'All You Need is Love'.

As the brides walked down the aisle and downhill back towards the hospitality tents by the castle entrance, the guests took pictures of them whist throwing biodegradable petal confetti over them. Amelia towered over Tara, but they seemed blissfully happy holding hands.

When Diana looked around at her other sister Aphrodite, she saw that she too was holding hands with her new friend Sian. She smiled. Perhaps that was why Aphrodite had never found the right man. It seemed that she also needed to find the right woman.

The caterers served bucks fizz as the guests filed past the brides and their families to congratulate them. Aphrodite was still holding hands with her girlfriend as the other guests passed by them.

The photographer called up the various family groups and friends' groups to get the best pictures she could. She had a young assistant who was flying a camera drone up and down to catch the best angles. The castle backdrop plus the guests and band turned out to be the best view of the day and stayed as Tara's Facebook header image for a long time afterwards.

When all the photographs were done, it was time for the wedding lunch.

The top table had to be slightly rearranged to accommodate Aphrodite's new beau – or should that be belle – next to her. Diana sat next to her husband and a little away from her sisters.

There were no big revelations during the speeches. Everybody was nice about each other. Tara thanked Diana and Stan for coming along so soon after the birth of their baby Ruby. And Diana was encouraged to stand up and show off Ruby to the guests, who gave the baby a round of applause.

The toasts to the bride and bride were made, and the various courses were served out. There were chicken and vegan tofu main courses as a buffet followed by jam roly-poly with custard. There was a gluten-free option, but it seems that this was Tara's favourite pudding from her school days.

At the end of the meal, the food was cleared away, and a dance floor was put in place over the grass inside the main tent.

As that was happening, the two brides threw their bouquets of matching yellow and purple crocus flowers into the crowd behind them. An already well-oiled Aphrodite and her girlfriend Sian caught both of the bouquets. Aphrodite shouted out "This time next year, stay tuned!"

Diana sighed. "Not again!"

The first dance, of course, was reserved for the two brides, but they were nowhere to be seen. They ran back panting wearing matching hot pink tops and tight leggings in the style of the girls from 'Grease'.

Sure enough, the first tune was 'Summer Nights' from the movie soundtrack, with Tara and Amelia singing along.

The disco then came out with many of the classic tunes from Tara's gay club outings in the 1990s and early 2000s.

The celebrations went on until nightfall and the time that the castle grounds had to close. At that point, a stretched white limousine arrived as close to the castle grounds as it was able to get. The two brides had brought up their suitcases when they went back to change, so got the chauffeur to place them in the boot of the car. They then got in as the guests threw what remaining confetti they had at them. The car then sped off with horns blowing, the just married signs on the back window, heading off for destination unknown.

Diana turned to Stan and gave him a big hug and a kiss. "Back to normality, I guess, whatever that is."

No sooner had she said that then the figure of Tallulah appeared from the other side of the bridge. In the coloured lights of the disco, her slim frame and Givenchy jacket with jeans set her apart from the other revellers.

"Hello, Diana, Stanislav and this must be Ruby?"

"Yes, that's correct," Diana replied, cooly.

"Thank you for your discretion at the press conference back in Miami. It was all for the greater good."

"Really?" Replied Diana.

"Yes. We are on the same side. We both want the truth to come out and for us to stay alive in this dangerous world. Well, you will be pleased to know that one of my pseudoscientific writer friends has just penned a book about his theories on Atlantis with just enough of your real Cuban scan evidence to drop another nugget into the hands of the public. It's a step forward that should allow you to make the announcement you wanted to back in Miami round about the time you both retire. I brought you a copy as a present for you and your baby. Enjoy!"

And with that, she turned around and left as suddenly as she had arrived.

A few minutes later, Diana and Stan left the party to take Ruby and themselves back to their lodgings. As Diana passed a bin, she casually dropped the book, 'Wrath of the Gods', into it.

XXVIII – Lines

That night, as Ruby and Stan slept, Diana had a dream.

A year after settling in the village in Peruvia, the Shaman-Healer Messima and her companion Néma were permitted to take a concubine of their own. Sidma was the son of the new chief Selema. She had become chief on the death of her mother. A poisonous snake had crept into the woman's tent and bitten her during her sleep. By the time she was discovered the next morning, it had been too late. Even with Messima's attempts to revive her, it had been the end for the older woman. As was customary her youngest daughter had been proclaimed the new Chief as her mother was cremated upon the funeral pyre. The sons of the new chief were bonded or married to the single women of the tribe to help ensure the survival of the clan. So it had been decided between Selema and Messima that Sidma would be bonded to her and Néma as joint possession. Néma was more reluctant to take a male lover but did crave a child of her own.

As the bonding ceremony was taking place, the embers of the funeral pyre were starting to die down. Torches had been lit, and a wild boar was being spit-roasted for the celebration.

Selema heated her ceremonial dagger of iron in flames then took each of the left hands of Sidma, Messima and Néma in turn and cut their palms with it. Then she got all three of them to grip their left hands together as tightly as they could to let the blood mingle. She then bound their hands with a vine to signify their mutual bonding. At the end of the ceremony, Messima and

Néma kissed before embracing Sidma as 'Bessma' – both concubine, husband and possession. He would now sleep in their tent and would have to protect them from any predators or rival tribes wanting to do them harm.

As the feasting began, some strange lights appeared in the sky and overflew the mountains in a triangular formation before climbing very fast and disappearing into the stratosphere. Messima had a brief feeling of dis-ease as they appeared before calming down as the lights went completely. She knew that it had been The Watchers and that they had left for good. The last message she had received from The Waterman was that there would be followers of the Annunaki left on Earth who would only be defeated at the end of the material age to come. He had also previously told her to persuade the tribe to move southwards as the Ice Age had ended and the lush hilltops that the tribe hunted in would become too hot and inhospitable.

At the end of the feasting, the brides and groom were ushered to their large hut where they would all consummate their bond. It was a new experience for all of them, but they grew to accept and even enjoy their intimacies. However, Sidma often found himself sleeping alone in the other cot as Néma and Messima kept up their relationship.

As the months went by both women fell pregnant. The game that the tribe depended upon were themselves migrating south more and more, and the diet of the tribe was becoming largely plant-based from the tapioca found within the forest.

Messima and Néma had become highly proficient midwives. Under their guidance, the death of babies and infants had virtually ceased except for an occasional stillbirth. So when their times came to give birth to their offspring, they were more than ready to share the experience. Néma's daughter Brinda was born in late November, followed by Messima's daughter on the morning of the December solstice. Being born to the Shaman on the solstice, Messima was persuaded that her daughter should take her name – Messima. Thereafter the first-born daughter of the Shaman would be named Messima.

As winter approached, it was decided that the tribe would migrate to the south. They would follow the mountain streams and live on the fish that were found in the water as they made their way towards the coastal plain many days travel from their village.

Messima carried little Messima on her back in a comfortable sling woven from wool from the alpacas that were found near to the village. The tribe had started to domesticate the animals long before the arrival of the Atlanteans. But it had been Messima who persuaded them to make use of the handy creatures for the task ahead to carry their belongings to their new settlement. Néma also carried her dark-eyed, dark-haired baby Brinda on her back in her papoose.

The half-sisters looked quite similar to each other apart from Messima junior's piercing blue eyes and white hair. Their father Sidma was a good scout. Alongside his cousin Zed the young men were able to spot danger and keep the party safe. They had managed to navigate around a rival tribe's village under cover of darkness without alerting them to their presence. Another time a lynx had crept into their camp and killed one of the alpacas. Sidma and Zed had been able to locate the lynx and scare it away from the party before it made any more attacks on them. They lit the tips of their spears that they had covered in tree resin and threw them at the lynx and her cub to persuade her to hunt elsewhere.

After some weary few weeks of travel, the tribe arrived at the edge of the coastal plain with the Pacific Ocean in the distance to the west. The Nazca plain itself was desolate and inhospitable, but the mountains were lush and green with plentiful grasslands for the alpacas to graze and fields of maize gently swaying in the light breeze. There was an adequate water supply, but it appeared that it could be seasonal as it came from meltwater in the high mountains.

The tribe soon set to work to build their settlement here.

Selema allowed Messima and Néma to organise the tribe to build the new village. With tribal knowledge and some Atlantean ingenuity, the new settlement was able to be made at the very edge of the fertile area. Irrigation channels were dug out to expand the area of crops into the arid plain itself. Some aqueducts were also built.

The new village was constructed out of fired mud bricks in a grid pattern around a central square. The huts themselves were square rather than round and were another hybrid concept that fused local materials, tribal building skills and Atlantean technology. There may not have been crystals here to light and power their houses, but their rooves were watertight and kept warm in winter.

As the village developed and prospered into an agrarian town stead, Messima continued to be the Shaman-Healer alongside her young daughter. Néma with her daughter plus her son, who was born in the town, concentrated on developing the agriculture of the area. Wild tomatoes, peppers and chillies were discovered in the hills as Sidma and Zed used their scouting skills to find more sources of food for the tribe. Potatoes or 'Earth Mothers' as they became known were discovered under one of the plants that had been mistakenly planted as a tomato. A child had become quite ill after eating it. Messima had been shown one of the fruits by the boy's mother. She had realised it was the poisonous fruit of the potato plant. The boy was given a herbal poultice for his stomach and made to drink plenty of water. The plants themselves were isolated from the others and replanted in a separate field.

With the onset of Brinda's first reproductive cycle, the young girl was nominated to be Selema's successor as chief. A great feast was held in the town square to celebrate. In honour of her family's Atlantean side, the settlement was named 'Medina' after their former home. Members of the tribe were allowed to go up in one of the alpaca skin hot air balloons that Néma had constructed to aid her in setting out the fields and buildings of the city.

On the last balloon ride, an ageing Néma took her wife up to show her a special surprise. As the balloon reached tens of metres in the air, Messima could make out the shape of a monkey set out in the dusty plain of Nazca. Neither woman had seen a monkey since they had left Atlantis for the last time many years ago. Long lines stretched out many kilometres into the distance, lightly etched into the desert plain.

Medina continued to prosper over many years. Selema became elderly then passed away in her sleep of old age. Her granddaughter Brinda became queen of Medina. Selema's body was embalmed and preserved in a vault at the edge of the town, as had been agreed by the council of elders with her blessing. Néma also succumbed to a chill that Messima could not cure with her healing knowledge. Only the dolphins could have saved her, she thought.
"Goodbye, my love. I do not think it will be long before I join you." Messima lit the flames to consume her best friend, wife, lover, companion and concubine. She acknowledged the Atlantean traditions and gave thanks to Amun-Ra with the Great Invocation. The temple that had been Néma's final project was a fitting place for her funeral pyre to be lit. It was a modest stepped pyramid reminiscent of the magnificent smooth monument once present in Atlán. The Priestess was once more at the Temple of the Sun. The Temple to the Moon was being

constructed at the other side of the town square.

That evening Messima hugged Sidma and took to her bed. In the morning, little Messima brought her mother a beaker of herbal tea as she had done for many years. But this time her mother did not wake as she set it down.

Diana awoke from her dream. A tear rolled down her cheek. Stan wiped it off and kissed her.

The End

Diana Garry will return in 'The Heiress'

Epilogue

Juggling family commitments and her job was still relatively new to Doctor of Archaeology Diana Garry. It used to be work before all else. But that was no longer possible. At least a short dig season to rescue a possible Celtic temple of Bridget from the developers who were turning the industrial waterside of Belfast into luxury flats should be straightforward enough. No mythical cities or dashing knights here next to Harland and Wolf's remaining shipyard. She chuckled to herself as she thought 'unless I was on the *Titanic* in a past life!' She had never had a great fear of water so that could certainly be discounted.

Acknowledgement

My thanks go out to Tiras Verey for producing such excellent cover graphics for this book and the others.

Thanks also need to go to Annie for her initial proofreading. I am sure that the final text is all the stronger for her checking it.

Thanks also to my many friends who humour me over my love for the legend of Atlantis.

Thanks to Sue, Dawn, Steve and my other friends who revived my interest in crystals and skull babies.

And thanks to Philippe for writing such an enthusiastic Forward.

Glossary

Atlán – The capital city of Atlantis with its distinctive concentric rings of islands around a central plaza. The main ports were situated just outside the capital at the junctions with the four great rivers

Atlantis Minor - modern-day Antarctica but before it was covered with ice, and when it was not at the South Pole

Crystal Cutter – a crystal powered ship whose silhouette we would describe as being similar to a Greek galley or a Viking longship, both its linear descendants

Crystalmancer – a specialist geologist who doused and searched for the best seams of crystal formations deep under the ground.

Crystal Stack – the primary power source within Atlantis, networked together and also used to enhance telepathic communication

Great River Delta – The River Plate in modern-day Argentina. Not inhabited and generally feared by Atlanteans

Joslin's disturbing dark image of a figure standing in a state of heightened anguish we might equate it to 'The Scream.'

Natural Hot Spring water – geothermal water piped across Atlantis to households from underground volcanic springs

Orichalcum – a very golden brass alloy used as a cheaper substitute to gold. Its modern-day counterpart would be 'Composition Gold Leaf' or Schlagmetal - imitation gold leaf made from brass and a combination of copper and zinc, but much thicker

Peruvia – Peru, Chile, Ecuador – a wide coastal strip of modern-day western South America. The Amazon and the East Coast

were not inhabited by Atlantean colonists.

Pillars of Heracles/Hercules – Gibraltar. Atlantis was clearly described as being beyond them in the Atlantic rather than in the Mediterranean.

Tuning Rods – used as an aid in tuning into crystal stacks, in much the same way that a suitable aerial strengthens a radio signal in our modern world today

Turtle Shell Lacquer – natural polish made from turtle shells cast-offs from turtles found off of Antarctica

Further Reading

Atlantis: The Antediluvian World by Ignatius Donnelly

Edgar Cayce's Atlantis by Gregory Little and John Van Auken

The Skull Chronicles series by D K Henderson (Fiction)

Critias by Plato

Timaeus by Plato

About The Author

Amethyst Gray

 Amethyst Gray was born on the Isle of Wight, England and grew up close to Carisbrooke Castle. The Island, Arthur C. Clarke's Mysterious World on TV, fossils on the beach and crystals gave her a keen interest in history, hidden history and how everything came about. She was always good at Mathematics, so ended up taking a Physics degree at the University of London. That led to a career in IT before rediscovering her interest in crystals, alternative history and energy healing after moving to Wiltshire in the early 2010s.

Now as well as being accomplished in IT, Amethyst teaches Angelic Reiki, practices Access Bars, Future Life Progression and Past-Life Regression in the vicinity of Avebury stone circle.

She has given lectures on Atlantis and is in the process of publishing her Diana Garry book series

The Diana Garry Book Series

Diana Garry is a doctor of Archaeology at Bath Sulis University in the south-west of England.

In her 30's, she has long given up on the idea of romance in her life. She has one passion and that is her Archaeology. Diana has specialities in the Phoenicians, Celts and Romans.

The world is a straightforward and straightforward place, as is its history. Everybody knows and accepts that. Modern history started with the adoption of agriculture in around 9000 BCE in the fertile crescent around the middle east that today includes northern Egypt, Israel, Jordan, Syria and Iraq. The ancient Sumerians, Babylonians, Assyrians, Egyptians, and Phoenicians were all responsible for the development of civilisation as we know it.

People and events can be categorised as religious and irrational or logical and scientific. Everything can be explained by science. Or so she thought.

In the Diana Garry book series, we follow Diana as her rigid belief systems are challenged in every possible way.

The Huntress

In 'The Huntress' Diana must confront her belief that reincarnation is a new-age idea gleaned from the far east without any basis on truth. She will glimpse the past, but not in an era that she is comfortable with. And her relationships in her own life go

in an unexpected, but welcome direction.

The Priestess

In 'The Priestess' a more mature and happier Diana is brought in on a dig that always had the possibility of challenging Columbus or the Vikings as the first visitors to the Americas from the Old World. But its ultimate conclusions – about Atlanatis - could challenge her more fundamental tenets. Will Diana get through this in one piece?

The Heiress

In 'The Heiress' a simple rescue dig finds a more relaxed and open-minded Diana once more challenged by the history she knows and loves compared with the evidence and visions she sees in front of her.

Printed in Great Britain
by Amazon

87710695R00103